A CLASS ACTION

Peter Sharp Legal Mystery #3

By Gene Grossman

From Magic Lamp Press
Venice, California

www.LegalMystery.com

This is a work of fiction. Any resemblance to actual persons, living or dead is entirely coincidental.

A CLASS ACTION
Peter Sharp Legal Mystery #3

This book, or parts thereof, may not be reproduced in any form, stored in a retrieval system, or transmitted by any means, electronic, mechanical, by photocopying, recording, or otherwise, without written permission from the publisher, Magic Lamp Press. For written permission, contact: Magic Lamp Press, P.O. Box 9547, Marina del Rey, CA 90295.

Peter Sharp Legal Mystery Series
http://www.LegalMystery.com

ISBN: 1-882629-66-3

The Complete
Peter Sharp Legal Mystery Series

www.LegalMystery.com

Single Jeopardy

By Reason of Sanity

A Class Action

Conspiracy of Innocence

...Until Proven Innocent

The Common Law

The Magician's Legacy

The Reluctant Jurist

The Final Case

An Element of Peril

A Good Alibi

Legally Dead

How to Rob a Bank

1

If you search the world over, I don't think you'll find any guy who will admit to being a bad driver. That's what makes me so unique. The general consensus of my neighbors here in Marina del Rey is that I am one of the worst drivers in the world, and to be honest, I really can't argue with them.

This is partly due to the fact that I have very shallow depth perception, which means I can't judge distances very well. It's also partly because I've grown accustomed to driving my old, small Mazda 626 - but now I'm driving a big Yellow Hummer. This is a big change for me and I'm having a really tough time getting used to it. This difficulty got pointed out to me one day last month when I drove little Suzi to turn in her quarterly home-schooling exams. I'm her legal guardian since her stepfather passed away, and she gave me a hint about my driving by sitting in the Hummer's back seat, strapping herself in, and putting on an adult-sized football helmet. As an adorable Chinese girl who doesn't speak that much to me, she's been known to express her feelings in more graphic ways.

During my former marriage to the county's newly elected District Attorney, we also had a nice luxury car that was used for going out in the evening.

1

She always drove. In some ways, I miss my old Mazda… and my ex-driver.

Due to the miraculous improvement in my income from the practice of law, I now have the real car of my dreams, but there's always some schmuck with a clipboard walking around, and one of them – one of my underground garage neighbors, complained to the Marina office about my driving skills. As a result, I now also rent the other two parking spaces on both sides of mine, so that nearby vehicles might be less likely to get banged by my yellow tank.

Having three parking spaces under the building is good and bad. It's bad because I have to pay extra for the other two spaces, but it's good because now there are fewer cars that can park between my spaces and the four reserved for George Clooney's limo. I've been told that his multi-million dollar megayacht is on the end-tie of our dock, and maybe now I'll have a better chance to bump into him and get friendly. After all, we are boat neighbors.

On the way back from turning in her test results, Suzi tells me she wants to make a stop on Pico Boulevard at a hobby shop just west of the Rancho Park Golf Course, so I park in front of the place while she goes in and purchases a two-foot-long, remote-controlled motor yacht. I've already learned not to ask questions about anything she does, because as the managing partner of her late step-father's law firm, technically, she's my boss.

2

Her stepfather was an old classmate of mine from law school, and after my suspension and subsequent divorce, he helped get me a slip near his houseboat for an old wooden Chris Craft that I was restoring and illegally living aboard. After he was killed in a plane crash and I was reinstated to practice again, I took his place in the law firm and then discovered that little Suzi was really the brains behind the whole operation. Not only is she a computer genius, she's also the star of a Chinese Restaurant around the corner where her late mother used to work. Most of the cops in our neighborhood eat lunch there every day and they've adopted her as their mascot, so we have no problem getting police reports and other little favors that most other law firms would kill for.

While Suzi practices driving her new mini motor yacht, the UPS man delivers a package for her. She must have ordered some instructional videos to help her master the art of boat handling because the package is from BOATINGDVD.COM. It isn't until several days later while talking to some of our dock neighbors that I learn what motivated Suzi to start her maritime education efforts. Our anchorage is getting concerned with legal liability for damages caused by inexperienced people driving their boats. Unlike automobiles, there's no age or experience required to drive a boat... and these big floating trucks don't have brakes.

It's hard to stop that industrial executive from getting behind the wheel of his yacht on Sunday and taking it for a spin, even though he hasn't had more than two hours of instruction given to him by the guy who sold him the boat, and told him "it's easier than driving a car."

People don't realize that a fifty-foot boat like ours, weighing almost forty tons, has a lot of force behind it, even at only two or three miles per hour. When it bumps into another half-million dollar boat, the damages cost a lot more to repair than Emilio charges at the local body shop. You can't just slap on some bondo and send one of these yachts to Earl Scheib for a paint job.

The new Marina rules require each boat to have a valid policy of liability insurance in place, and the owner must take the Coast Guard Auxiliary's boating safety course and pass their test. In addition to these requirements, our anchorage demands that the dockmaster watch every boat's owner pull in and out of the slip, to judge their boat handling abilities.

I guess that because my non-existent boat-driving ability has caused a vacuum of respect, the job of satisfying the new Marina boat owners' requirements has been taken over by the kid. I don't want to be around to see her try to get this huge boat in and out of the slip. I know that I certainly can't do it. I think I'll concentrate on developing my driving skills on land before trying to drive our fifty-foot Grand Banks trawler yacht. In contrast, my driving experience doesn't look too bad when compared with what happened to a soccer mom today.

Tonight's local news has a story about a big GMC Suburban that blew up. Fortunately there were no serious injuries. The owner picked it up at the dealership after some routine service was performed, and drove it all around town, until there was a loud 'bang,' the engine died, and the hood flew off. No foul play is suspected, but there's surely going to be some lawyer getting involved in this... it's too strange an event to be ignored by our bottom-feeding legal community – the shysters at law.

My evening television news viewing is interrupted by a call from Vinnie Norman, a former client and present associate of my good friend Stuart Schwarzman, who is the most entrepreneurial guy I know. After getting rich off of the publicity he got from being sued for 'negligent nymphomania' when a user of a weight loss product he sells claimed to have been turned into a nymphomaniac, he went on to start several other businesses. His most profitable is the one that accepts assignments of small court claims from people who have received unsolicited 'junk' faxes. Stuart uses a recently enacted Federal Law call the TCPA, to sue those senders for five hundred dollars on each claim, and splits the recoveries with his client.

Stuart also bought an old Brinks armored truck and changed the outer signage to read: *'HE'S TAKING IT WITH HIM.'* He rents the truck and a driver out to disgruntled heirs for three hundred fifty dollars: they pay to have the truck drive behind the hearse that takes their tightwad deceased to the cemetery. Vinnie drives one of the trucks for Stuart and Vinnie's fiancée Olive will be driving the second one soon.

Stuart paid for both Olive and Vinnie to get firearm training so that they could be issued Exposed Firearm Permits by the Department of Consumer Affairs. Now they can wear holstered but unloaded weapons with their uniforms when they drive the phony armored trucks in funeral processions. Everyone in this town is in showbiz.

Vinnie's current problem is causing quite a crisis in his house. After Stuart spent all that money getting Vinnie and Olive outfitted and armed, and then buying another armored truck for Olive to operate, she confessed to Vinnie that she has a slight problem when it comes to operating the truck. She never learned how to drive.

It would have been a lot nicer if Vinnie could have had that information before, because now he fears that when Stuart finds out, his own job might be in jeopardy.

After listening to his desperate babbling for about fifteen minutes, I learn that Stuart's second armored truck won't be ready for another month or so. This means that Olive may have time to take some driving lessons and get licensed in time for her first funeral job. I don't think there's any way in hell that she'll pull it off. I know that I couldn't learn to drive that armored truck in only a month or so, and I've been driving poorly for over twenty-five years.

I wish him luck, get off the phone and start to prepare the evening meal. The special tonight will be my 'pasta ala Marina.' The only thing I know how to do is boil water and cook pasta, so my recipe repertoire consists of numerous large elbow macaroni dishes.

One fan of my cooking is Bernie, Suzi's huge Saint Bernard, who also lives with us on the boat. Whenever he sees me start to prepare some food he's at my feet the entire time, hoping for some droppings. This evening I'll be making my version of a healthy Alfredo sauce, using *Land-O-Lakes* non-fat half and half, *Kraft* non-fat grated Parmesan cheese, *Smart Beat* trans-fat-free butter, and some *Knudsen* fat-free sour cream.. As the secret ingredient, I'll be adding a new salt-free garlic salt. The result may be non-taste sauce, but at least it'll be healthy.

All of these allegedly healthy ingredients have been mandated by Suzi, who now peeks out from her domain – the foreward stateroom, when she smells the aromas. I can usually tell by her expression whether or not I'm on the right track with my formula.

Most of the time a gourmet Chinese meal gets delivered to the boat by the Asian boys, a group of young Chinese teenagers who do everything from wait on and bus tables at the local Szechwan restaurant, to varnish and maintain boats on our dock. Like most of the other people in this Marina, they adore Suzi, so one way or another I manage to have a tasty dinner.

We usually have special nights designated during each week; one for my pasta special, one for entertaining guests, one for eating out, and the others for having the Asian boys serve us dinner. Tonight it's pasta. The word must have gotten out about my new recipe, because Stuart calls to tell me he's on the way over. Suzi must have invited him after approving the bouquet wafting toward her stateroom.

I'm sure that Stuart made the initial call and wormed the invitation out of her. Now that he's signed up with some correspondence mail-order law school, he's her prize student. If not for the fact that you have to be twenty-one years old to practice law in California, she wouldn't need me at all. She runs the law practice, prepares the pleadings, does all the legal research, and pays me quite well to do her bidding in court. The other reason she can't practice law now is because she isn't tall enough to see over the counsel tables in the courtroom. When taking over as her legal guardian, I was concerned that she wasn't attending one of the local public schools. I now know that several years ago Melvin received permission for her to be home-schooled. All she has to do is go downtown every month or so to pass the Board of Education's home-schooling exams. The strange thing now is that instead of teachers coming to visit her, all I see are people coming to learn from her.

When Stuart gets to the boat he's bubbling over with his new business idea - a used car lot. I tell him that if he's looking for respect, he's going in the wrong direction. It's bad enough that he wants to be a lawyer, because there are very few jobs that rank lower in the public's scale of esteem, but used car salesman is one of them.

He explains to me that the chance to make a great profit here is too good to pass up. He owns his own warehouse in the San Fernando Valley, where he has his weight-reduction products stored and his armored trucks garaged. There's also a large enough parking lot for him to qualify for a used car sales permit, so he's going for it.

I point out to him that he's not in an area where any other car lots are, and ask him where he's going to get the cars to sell and the customers to buy them. As usual, his answer is quite remarkable.

"Peter my dear friend, you have hit the nail right on the head. Getting customers is no problem if you offer the right product at the right price – and I can do it. I've made an arrangement with I.R.S..."

"Stuart, you're not working with the government on this deal are you?"

"No, no, no. This I.R.S. stands for a New Jersey company named Insurance Recovery Sales. There's a lot of auto theft in New York, and if an insured car isn't recovered within a thirty-day period, the insurance company must pay the policy holder. If the car is subsequently recovered, the insurance company dumps it as soon as possible to these I.R.S. guys, and I can buy the cars for a little over half of the wholesale blue book."

"I don't know, Stu, you know what they say about a deal that's too good to be true..."

"Yeah Pete, I know, but I've been to New Jersey and saw their warehouse, and believe me, this deal is true."

There's no talking him out of it, so I do what I usually do every time he comes up with one of his new business ideas – wish him the best of luck and let him know that I'll be available if he needs any help.

Not too long ago, I settled his uncle's wrongful death suit. He and Suzi's stepfather both died when their plane crashed during take-off from some local airport in Thailand, where they were vacationing. That's why both Stuart and the kid are the richest people I know - until I bump into my neighbor, George.

With no important cases going on, it's time for a little relaxation, so I'm going to walk over to the Marina del Rey Junior Liquor Store to pick up a six-pack, a box of our neighbor's favorite wine, and a Playboy. On the way there, I'll stop by Laverne's boat.

The Marina has several boxy houseboats they rent out and Laverne lives in one that's on our dock. At one time she probably was a real looker, but all the looking she does now is out of the window of her houseboat, waiting for me to walk by so she can clink two wine glasses together and wink at me. I call it the 'wink and clink,' but clink probably isn't the proper word, because the glasses are plastic. They just sort of clunk.

On several occasions I've allowed myself to be led astray and spent the night aboard with her. Aside from the 'early whorehouse' décor, it's a comfortable place, and she never fails to leave some greasy French toast out for me the next morning when she goes to work.

I still don't know what she does for a living, but some husky guy picks her up every morning at seven and brings her back at six each evening. She may have a couple of years on my forty-three, but she keeps herself well-preserved in alcohol, so the deterioration's been minimal.

My plan is to stop by her boat, tell her I'm going to the market, and ask her if there's anything she needs. It's starting to get dark. I politely knock on her boat. She pops her head out of the window and after my announcement, requests some crackers and a bag of ice.

Knowing I'm in for some greasy French toast tomorrow morning, I rush to the liquor store and back. As expected, upon my return, the wink and clink are my signal to 'come aboard.' We finish off that box of wine and spend prime time watching one of those stupid reality shows that she likes. She's been known to tape an episode when not around to watch it live, making for an extremely elegant video library. The only books she has on board are some romance novels, each one showing a Fabian wannabee on the cover, shirt torn half off, and a desperate nymphet hanging on him. Every time I go to the neighborhood Ralph's Market I see those soap-opera paperbacks. I used to wonder what type of desperate person would spend their money on them.

Being only partially embalmed I can still see that the late news is showing an angry man threatening to bring a lawsuit against the dealership where his wife's Suburban was serviced. I assume that's the one that exploded.

After the wine and the news we retreat to the aft stateroom part of her floating trailer and fumble ourselves asleep.

It must be about two in the morning and I'm suddenly awake, sensing someone heavy creeping onto her houseboat. Whoever it is stops near the bedroom. I quietly sneak over to the window to get a look outside, and when I stick my head out the window, I hear a low whine. It's Suzi's huge Saint Bernard. When he sees me, he stands up against the side of the boat and I notice that my cell phone is hanging around his neck. I remove it and the dog goes back to our boat. The cell phone is turned on. After holding it for a minute or so, trying to figure out what the hell is going on, it rings.

It's FBI Special Agent Bob Snell, head of the West Los Angeles office. Not too long ago, I was instrumental in getting some information together on a gang of bank robbers, and Snell made the arrests - and took the credit. The reward money was a big contribution to the purchase of our present fifty-foot Grand Banks, so I guess you could say we've got a decent working relationship.

"Hello Sharp, are you there? It's Bob Snell… special agent Bob Snell, FBI."

"Yeah Snell, I'm here. What's the matter, you guys working overtime tonight? It's kinda late."

"I know it's late Sharp, but the reason I'm calling now is because I'd like to ask you a favor."

"I'm listening."

"Well this is kind of embarrassing, but one of our people has been arrested. We were at a party tonight honoring the retirement of a Federal Agent we all respect. After we left, one of our associates got arrested for drunk driving. She's being held in the Van Nuys LAPD Jail."

"That's a sad story, but I still don't know why you're calling me at two in the morning."

"We'd like to get her out of jail."

"So, why call me? Call a bail bondsman. They can get her out in no time. Got a pencil? Call Fradkin Bail Bonds. Their number is four seven eight,…'

He cuts me off mid-sentence. "No, no, no. We can't use a bail bondsman."

"Why not?"

"Because we're FBI agents. If the press ever found out we used a bondsman to bail out a member of the Federal Anti-Crime Task Force, they'd have a field day with it."

"So? What do you want me to do?"

"Her bail is twenty-five hundred dollars and we don't have that much cash – and they won't accept a check. We have about five hundred between

13

us. If you can lend us two thousand, I'll give you my personal check for it, right on the spot. And don't worry, the check is good."

"Boy, what a deal. You'll take my hard-skimmed two grand and turn it into a check that I'll have to deposit and report on my income tax. What're you trying to do, make an honest person out of me?"

"Sorry Sharp, but I'm afraid that ship's already sailed. Look, can you help us out or not?"

I know for a fact that most first time offenders don't have to post bail because they get released on their own recognizance, just like a traffic ticket that the cop asks you to sign. He doesn't want your autograph. He wants you to sign a promise to appear in court. What you are receiving at that time is what they call a field 'R.O.R.,' an acronym for Release on your Own Recognizance.

If I call up and talk to the Van Nuys watch commander and let him know that he's got a fed in his house, I'm sure I can get her an R.O.R.

"Okay Snell, tell you what. You and your partner meet me at the Van Nuys Jail in forty-five minutes. And when we get there, just walk with me and don't say anything. When we get to the officer at the front desk, just flip your ID's at him and have a seat in the lobby. Got it?"

"Okay, you're in charge. We'll see you there."

I call Van Nuys and explain what's going on to the watch commander. Fortunately he remembers my name, because last year I helped his boss out on a case. He tells me that the girl in custody is still pretty much out of it and he doesn't want to see her driving so soon. I assure him that she's going to be picked up by two FBI agents who will be identifying themselves at the front desk. He agrees to have her ready to go by the time we get there.

Forty-five minutes later I meet Snell and another fed outside the jail. It looks like a drug deal going down.

"Thanks for coming, Sharp. Did you bring the cash? I've got my checkbook right here."

"Don't be so hasty. You're in my ballpark now, so let's go upstairs and see if I can work some magic."

"What do you mean?"

"No questions. Just follow me and get ready to flip those fancy ID wallets when we walk in the front door."

They take my instructions and follow me up the stairs to the jail floor. As we enter the front door, there's a uniformed officer seated at a small table. I show him my State Bar card and nod to the Feds. They each flash their ID and as we walk into the waiting area, their eyes bulge out.

Only one person is sitting in the lobby. It's a disheveled female, probably in her early thirties. I ask Snell. "Is that her?"

He's totally amazed. There she is, sitting on a chair in the waiting lobby. No handcuffs, no guards, no security. "Yeah, that's her, that's Shirley."

I motion for her to come with us, and she walks over to meet Snell and his partner. She looks at me. "Am I free to go now?"

"Yes, you are. You can go with Agent Snell and his friend but you can't drive. They'll take you home and you can pick up your car tomorrow."

We all walk out together. "Sharp, I don't know how you did it, but we all thank you. Will she be going to court soon?"

I take a look at her R.O.R. papers and tell them when and where her court appearance is. She asks me for help on her case. Snell calls me aside.

"What's the deal with these drunk driving charges? Is there going to be a big fine?"

"Of course there is. Listen, my miracle working is limited. I can get someone out of jail occasionally, but there's no way I can make this drunk driving charge go away."

"Will she have to appear in court?"

"Someone's got to be there on her behalf. With the proper document signed, waiving her appearance right, an attorney can appear for her and enter a plea."

"Will you do it?"

"Yeah, I can represent her, but can she afford to pay a fee? You know, by the time the case is over the fine and court costs can add up to over a thousand dollars... but I can get her some time to pay that off."

"We can't have that."

"Whatta ya mean you can't have that? Who the hell do you think you are, The Federal Government?"

16

"No, no. What I mean is that if she gets a fine of anything more than twenty-five dollars, she'll lose her security clearance and get fired from her job. Can't you do something? How much is your fee?"

"Well, maybe something can be done. I charge a thousand to handle cases like this. I can see by the stunned expression on your face that you think it's a lot, so just make a check out to me for five hundred, and I'll represent her in court. The watch commander led me to believe that her Breathalyzer reading was way over the legal limit, so there'll probably be no reduction of the charge to reckless driving… but I'll talk to the judge."

Snell writes out a check to me for the five hundred dollars and makes sure to tell me that I should report it on my income tax. They all leave in his car and I go back to the Marina. Damn. Laverne is probably out like the lights on her boat, so now I won't get to earn my plate of greasy French toast for breakfast.

2

A dogmail instructs me to call attorney Charles Indovine. He's got a big law firm downtown that specializes in doing insurance defense work, and his biggest client is the Uniman Insurance Company, the firm that insures the car dealership where the exploding Suburban was serviced. True to his threats on the news broadcast, the owner of that vehicle is suing the dealership. The insurance company sent the file to Indovine's office and they decided to assign it to me. I did a favor for Mister Uniman last year, so no doubt he probably told Indovine to toss me a bone every once in a while.

The file is being brought over by messenger, along with a fifteen hundred dollar retainer check. Not bad. Two grand already in this week, with some new cases in the hopper. I haven't the slightest idea what to do with Shirley the fed's drunk driving case, but I sure know what to do with this one from Indovine's office: build up the hours. Indovine pays me one hundred per hour for my time, and I'm pretty sure he bills Uniman Insurance more than two fifty. That means his firm makes plenty of money on each hour I put in, so 'rush' is a word that's not in their vocabulary.

On the other hand, Shirley is in a hurry to get her case over with. If she only knew that the quicker it gets done the quicker she'll get fired, maybe she'd ask me to stall it along for a while.

While glancing through Indovine's file on the exploding Suburban, I see that the plaintiff's lawyer is contending that a certain popular legal principle is involved in this case. It has the fancy Latin name of *Res Ipsa Loquitur*, but a plain English translation is that it simply means 'the thing speaks for itself.'

Stuart mentioned he's studying that principle now in his correspondence law course and it's giving him some difficulty, so I invite him over for dinner later this week to discuss it, and to let him help me out on this file. It's about time he gets a feel for what a real lawyer does on a case – and I'm sure that Indovine won't mind my hiring a paralegal to help out. Usually Suzi gets the job, but she's so busy learning all about seamanship that she doesn't have any spare time this month. That's a good thing, because her hourly rate is thirty-five bucks, and I'm sure Stuart will work for half of that. Of course Suzi is smarter than both of us, but Stuart will do just fine, if he follows my instructions.

Shirley's arraignment date is this morning, and as I drive to the West Los Angeles Municipal Courthouse, I haven't the slightest idea of how to save her job.

The courtroom is packed with people. All the drunk drivers on the west side who were arrested last weekend are here for their arraignments today and their lawyers are lined up waiting for a chance to beg the courtroom's Deputy City Attorney for a reduction to reckless driving. If they're successful in getting the charge reduced, the fine will probably be the same but it's sure nice to be able to avoid having a drunk driving conviction on your record, because if you do it again, you'll be doing some mandatory jail time.

After about twenty minutes of pushing through the crowd, there's a brief opening at the prosecution's counsel table, so I walk over and introduce myself. She thinks she knows what I want. I wish she'd tell me, because at this time I don't know what I want.

"Hello, my name is Peter Sharp. I'm here on your case number 7875044." She looks up at me with a faint expression of recognition on her face.

"You're the D.A.'s ex, aren't you?"

"Please don't hold that against me... I just want to talk about this case."

"No, I mean you're the one that helped get her elected to the office... and my uncle, Mister Seymour, was put out of work."

"I'm sorry your uncle lost his job but he was only the acting District Attorney, and he..."

She's in no mood to talk to someone who forced her uncle out of work, and if I was under any impression that I'd get some cooperation in this courtroom, she just proved me wrong.

"Excuse me, but I wonder if you could join me in chambers to discuss this case?"

She quickly goes through her file. "What for? There's no deal to be made here. She blew a one point four... that's almost twice the legal limit. She's going down."

"I know she is, but that's what I'd like to discuss with the judge… we've got a special situation here, and I can't get into it out here in the courtroom. Will you please join me in chambers? We both know that the judge won't talk to me unless you're there too, so I promise you right here and now that if you'll go into chambers with me, I'll plead her straight up to the drunk driving charge."

She hesitates for a minute and looks at her wristwatch. "Okay, I'll give you three minutes." She then signals the court clerk to buzz the judge and let him know we're on the way to his chambers.

Judge Parker is a former Deputy Attorney General who prosecuted many Federal crimes before getting appointed to the bench. Because he was a fed himself, I'm hoping he'll understand Shirley's special security clearance predicament and give me some way to go.

It was a tough decision offering to plead her guilty to the charge in the arraignment court, but I had to do it in order to get to this judge – a former fed.

When we get into chambers I once again am shown that that this deputy city attorney isn't giving an inch. "Your Honor, counsel's client blew a one-four, and he promised to plead her straight up, so I have no idea why we're in here."

The judge looks at me. "Counsel, perhaps you can give the City Attorney some reason why you're in here. She already told you there's no deal to be made, and you offered to plead your client straight up. So what's there to talk about?"

"Your Honor, my client is a federal employee. All I'm at liberty to say is that she's connected to the United States Attorney General's Organized Crime Task Force. Being a former fed yourself, you know what happens if a person gets convicted of anything that carries more than a twenty-five dollar fine."

"Yes I do counsel. She loses her security clearance and gets fired. But she should have thought of that before she drove drunk that night. She was a danger to herself and to others, and she deserves a conviction, whether she's a federal employee or not."

"I agree Your Honor, and she'll get one - that's what I promised the City Attorney. All I'm saying here is that if she loses her job, then maybe justice isn't served. I'm not on the list of people who get information on what that task force is working on, but whatever it is, the public will no doubt be much better off if they succeed, than if she loses her job. I'm not asking for any special favor like a dismissal or reduction to reckless driving here. All I want is for us to work out something with the fine."

The City Attorney puts her two cents in. "The fine on cases like this is less than four hundred dollars. The thing that gets it raised up to thirteen hundred is the addition of court costs and a penalty assessment. We can't do anything about that. If you want those numbers changed, you'll have to have the State Legislature do if for you. We don't do things like that here."

That doesn't help, but I really wasn't expecting anything better from her. Suddenly I get a brainstorm. If they go for it, maybe I'll make history – and at the same time keep my standing with the Feds as a genuine miracle worker.

"Okay, I'll tell you what. If I plead her guilty and the court gets its thirteen hundred, that's all you guys really care about right? I mean, will that make the City Attorney's office and the court happy?"

The judge is a smart cookie. It looks like he may know where I'm going with this. Now that I've got their attention, I might as well try to close the deal.

"Here's my suggestion. Why don't we make the fine twenty-five dollars and the court costs and penalty assessment total twelve hundred seventy-five? That way the City Attorney gets its conviction, the court gets the same total amount of money, but the money description gets shoved around a little, so my client can keep her job. And that will be a saving of more public money because she won't have to be on the people's dime for unemployment or welfare benefits."

The City Attorney looks at me with contempt on her face. She probably now realizes why her inept uncle is out of work – because he just didn't have the brainpower to compete with his opponent's campaign manager. She gives the standard civil service answer. "No, we can't do that. It's against the rules." I can't let that remark go unanswered so I tell her what my next suggestion is.

"I've got another great idea. This man sitting here is the judge. He makes the rules in this courtroom. What he says goes. So instead of you telling him what he can or can't do, why don't we let him be in charge of this disposition? I'm willing to go along with whatever he says. Are you?"

She doesn't answer that question. It looks like there's been some conflict between these two in the past. Prosecutors sometimes have a feeling that because they represent the People, that they are the law. Some judges stand for it and others don't. I'm hoping that this judge, who was a former federal prosecutor, will stand his ground and not get pushed around by this dame.

There's silence in the room. The City Attorney is contemplating her navel. I'm staring right at the judge, letting him know that he's got to face me here and now with a decision. He steps up to the plate.

"Okay, counsel. I'll accept her plea. Twenty-five dollars for a fine and the rest as court costs and penalty assessment."

We both thank the judge and leave. I get to the cashier's desk and make arrangements for monthly payments on the total amount. The Federal Government owes me big time, but I know I'll never collect on this marker. You can ask any American Indian about how good the feds are at keeping promises.

Stuart shows up on time for dinner and we all look forward to the gourmet dinner that's being brought over to the boat.

After he gets the kid to help him fill out the forms for his used car dealer's license bond, we sit down to enjoy the Chinese feast that was delivered and is now being served up by the Asian boys. During dinner, Stuart starts to expound on Res Ipsa Loquitur by telling me that it's a meaningless concept because everything speaks for itself. Now the lively debate starts. "Peter, when you see one car with its rear end smashed in and another right behind it with its front end smashed in, doesn't that sort of speak for itself? I mean, that's a rear-ender and there's no getting out of it."

"Maybe Stu. I'll admit that the fact of the two of them colliding speaks for itself, but it doesn't necessarily say which one of them was negligent. What if the car in front caused the damages by backing up into the car behind it?" That's not good enough for him. He keeps arguing his point.

"So what? The fact still remains that they collided and both got smashed up. That speaks for itself, doesn't it?"

"Yes, but it's not just a factual statement that you want to speak for itself. You want to use the doctrine to replace two of the elements of a negligence case."

"Oh yeah I know. The four elements are Duty, Breach, Causation, and Damages."

"Very good, Stu. In that rear-ender you described, the breach of one person's duty to drive their car carefully certainly caused damages to the other driver, but we really don't know which breached the duty. Did the guy in back rear-end the car in front or did the guy in front front-end the car in back?"

"Okay, professor, if you're so smart, why don't you give me a perfect example of that Latin mumbo-jumbo and let me know how it has anything to do with that case you got assigned from the defense firm."

"All right Stuart, here goes. A person has an operation at the hospital. Next day the patient feels some discomfort in her side. They X-ray her and discover that there's a surgical tool someone forgot to take out of her body during the recent surgery."

Everyone in the room winces at the thought of this terrible possibility. "I know it sounds horrible, but if it did happen that way, the patient's lawyer can use the doctrine of Res Ipsa to avoid the necessity of proving up the duty and breach portions of the negligence case, because the fact that there is a surgical instrument inside the client's body shortly after surgery speaks for itself. The only thing the lawyer might have to do is show a picture of the client's X-ray prior to the surgery, to establish that she didn't have that surgical instrument in there to begin with, because in that case, the doctors might only be sued for missing it in the first X-ray." Stuart is now rubbing his chin.

"Hmmm. Okay Peter, maybe that left-over scalpel does prove negligence, but it doesn't nail down who did it."

"It doesn't have to. All it does is speak for itself as to the fact that there has been some negligence. That's all the doctrine is supposed to do. After that, it's always the lawyer's job to place the blame that's already been established onto the responsible party."

"All right. I think I get it now. But please tell me exactly what the Suburban plaintiff's lawyer means by it."

"Simple Stuart – he's contending that the mere fact of the explosion so soon after the Suburban being serviced by experts on that type of vehicle speaks for itself too. There's no way the explosion could have been caused without the negligence of someone working at that dealership. Just like in the scalpel case, it doesn't nail down who was negligent... all he's contending is that for darn sure, *someone was* negligent."

All the while we're talking the television set is on, but with the volume muted, so as not to disturb our dinner conversation. We usually leave it on because the dog enjoys watching the pet food commercials. Suddenly Suzi picks up the TV remote and raises the volume so we can hear the local newsreader. "Well, folks, looks like we've got a strange situation here in West Los Angeles. Another Suburban serviced by that same dealership has exploded this evening. Fortunately it wasn't fatal, but the hood did blow off the vehicle, scaring the heck out of the driver. She's right over there. The paramedics have just finished up with her and I'm going over to interview her now..."

That was all I need to hear and Suzi knows it, because at that point she puts the volume back onto 'mute.'

"Well Pete, I guess that sort of speaks for itself too."

Stuart is right. This second explosion is much more than I ever expected. It raises too many questions. I've never heard about things like this happening before, so I'm mentally ruling out a design defect in that particular model of vehicle. The only other two remaining possibilities are that someone at that dealership is playing some really sick practical jokes, or it's merely a coincidence that two similar model vehicles both had explosions, shortly after being serviced at the same dealership.

It shouldn't take a Las Vegas odds-maker to figure out that it's probably not a coincidence.

3

Charles Indovine likes to make his calls bright and early in the morning. He's heard that the word on the street is about the same lawyer handling the first Suburban explosion having sent his investigator over to solicit the second owner as a client too. Now that the same guy represents them both, he's threatening to bring a class action against the dealership. I don't know much about class actions, but I would rather not have Indovine know about my inexperience.

"He must be crazy. I've heard of classes with as few as twenty people, but the court would never certify a class that had only two plaintiffs."

"Well, you might be correct there, Pete. The Numerosity requirement for class certification probably wouldn't be satisfied with just two, but we don't know how many more there might be out there. I spoke to Mister Uniman and we were thinking that this could present some extremely large liability exposure for the dealership, and we don't think you're equipped to handle it at this time. The case needs investigation and a lot of technical knowledge, and we don't know…"

"Hold on Charles. We went through this last time, when you guys wanted to yank that slip-and-fall wrongful death case from me, and I wound up saving Uniman over a million dollars. Please, let me look into this for another couple of days. If I can't find out anything useful, then you can have the case back."

Silence on the other end, for what seems like an hour. "Peter, we'll give you until the end of the week, but if your investigation hasn't come up with anything mitigating by then, we're going to assign it to our class action department. It's our duty to the client."

That was it. I got another couple of days out of him, so I call Jack Bibberman. He's helped me out of some real tough ones in the past, and I'm starting to rely on him like Nero Wolfe relied on Archie Goodwin. He's not the best investigator in the world, but he's a schleppy, non-threatening kind of guy who people feel comfortable with. Somehow he gets them to tell him things that no other cop or investigator would succeed in drawing out of people. Maybe it's because when they see him they spot a guy who's lower on the food chain then they are. If you look up failure in the dictionary, you should see a picture of Jack B. He can do anything but make a living – but I like him, and he always comes through for me.

Jack succeeds in getting interviews with the drivers of both Suburbans, and also obtains a list of all the dealership's employees. I remind myself to have Jack get a statement from Joe Morgan, the last mechanic to sign off on both of the Suburbans. I also wanted to know exactly where each of those vehicles was driven, so Jack got their exact routes for me and learned that they didn't explode on the same day they

31

were picked up from the service bay. It took at least a day or two of driving before each one blew its hood off. My next step is to follow their steps to try and see if there's any way that something might have been done to those vehicles after they left the dealership.

I hear the pitter-patter of big paws entering my stateroom. It's a dogmail for me. The kid's note reminds me to reset my odometer for every trip I make on this case so she can do precise billing. She'll be charging Indovine for my time and mileage when preparing the weekly statement sent to his office, and because this will probably be the last chance we have to get any money out of this case, she wants to make the most of it.

I read the message and wash my hands. I'm going to have to tell that kid to put future messages on his collar instead of in his mouth.

The next couple of days are spent going over witness statements and mapping out routes to follow. This is the end of the week, so if I don't come up with anything Indovine will be taking the case back. Maybe he's right. Class action defense requires a full staff of people to process all the paperwork, and I just don't have it. I'm going to take care of the last item on my check-list, so I go to the dealership and introduce myself to the assistant manager. When he finds out I'm on his side, he offers full cooperation. I tell him that I'm going to re-trace the routes driven by those two claimants and he surprises me with an offer.

"Hey, as long as you're trying to re-create their routes, why not drive the exact same kind of vehicle they were driving? I see you've got a big Hummer, so it shouldn't be any problem for you to drive a big Suburban."

I thank him and tell him that I really don't want to impose.

"Hey, no problemo. There's one right over there that was just serviced... and no customer can complain about your using it, because it's assigned to our general manager's wife... and she won't be here to pick it up until late this afternoon. You said you'll be back here by noon, so there shouldn't be any problem."

Why not? I take the keys and start out on my first route, with several pages printed out from Mapquest.com and the statements of both drivers. I know exactly where they went, what stores they stopped at, where they parked, and exactly where the explosions took place. Following instructions from Jack and Suzi, I created a logbook to record exact mileage and driving times. And just to play safe, I drive as slowly as traffic will allow. I don't want to cause too much of an accident if the hood of this thing gets blown off.

The trips were nothing special. The main thing I was looking for was any place that one of them might have stopped long enough to allow someone access to the engine compartment. The first driver's route went past the soccer field, probably to drop off the players, and then on to the other important places like a hairdresser, the Galleria, and a gourmet food store. Good thing that the kids were dropped off before the car exploded. If she had driven another few miles before picking them up, the Suburban would have been loaded with a girls' soccer team, and the hysterical screams would have been louder and more damaging than the explosion.

The other one's routine was similar, with the same types of stops. It seems to be the fad nowadays for husbands married to women barely five feet tall to get them huge trucks to drive. I guess they see some need to drive such big heavy vehicles to pick up the family's dry cleaning and groceries. But who am I to talk? I bought a huge Hummer mainly to drive a kid and a dog downtown a couple of times each year.

I bring the borrowed Suburban back to the dealership a little after one in the afternoon, make my final entries in the logbook, and look for the assistant manager to thank him for his cooperation. He's nowhere to be seen. I ask a salesman where the assistant manager is, and he tells me that the general manager was really pissed at him for letting me use his wife's vehicle. She'll be there in a couple of hours to get it.

That was unfortunate. I certainly didn't want to get the guy in any trouble.

Suzi figures the mileage and does the final billing for Indovine's office. I guess I'm out of the class action business for now. Whenever I'm in a down mood, I try to give myself a little gift. Tonight it'll be the unfinished business I left at Laverne's houseboat last time, so I walk over there to get the clink and wink.

As usual, we get comfortable, open a can of wine from her private reserve, and get into bed to watch the early evening news.

After the reports of car-jackings, bank robberies, and the results of last night's high-speed chases, the announcer has a news flash. "Just an hour ago, there was another explosion of a vehicle serviced at the same West Los Angeles dealership – but this time, there were two deaths... the wife of the dealership's general manager and her mother. The explosion didn't kill these women, but it forced the driver to lose control and the car flipped off of Mulholland Drive and down a steep two hundred foot embankment."

I may have quite a bit of cheap wine in me, but not too much to realize that those two women died in the same Suburban that I was driving earlier today.

4

What the hell could have happened to that Suburban between the time that I drove it and the time it blew up?

Any normal person in my place would probably think he just survived a close call, but I think not. There's got to be more involved here than a poorly designed vehicle. I hope that Indovine's high-priced class action department doesn't get sucked into giving away a lot of Uniman's insurance money to settle these cases, because something smells funny here. I make a mental note to drive the same route from the dealership to where this last car went off of Mulholland, just to check out the route between the dealership and there... but this time I'll be in my Hummer – no more borrowing cars from that dealership.

My phone doesn't stop ringing with calls from friends who knew I had been working on the dealership's defense. Stuart calls, but I refuse to argue any more with him about the applicability of Res Ipsa in these cases. The afternoon news reports that the class action has now been expanded to include the dealership's general manager as a plaintiff. He's also suing for wrongful death. Indovine's firm is going to make a lot of money on this one, but probably not as much as the insurance company will lose.

The reporter interviews my ex-wife, the newly elected District Attorney. She plays it safe, only saying that her department is looking into the double deaths and if any evidence of foul play is revealed, they'll turn it into a criminal investigation.

From the boat I can see into the lower level garage where the apartment tenants and boat-owners park, and it looks like someone is in my Hummer. When I go over to check, I see it's our techie dock neighbor Don Paige, and he's doing some wiring thing near the driver's seat. As usual, it's at the kid's instruction. She was unhappy with the way that I made entries in the logbook, so Don is installing a voice-activated recorder. All I have to do is glance at the odometer and dashboard clock and tell the device where I am, what time it is, and what the odometer reading is. She can then transcribe the recording and do her billing.

Don reminds me that I have to make sure that the recorder is turned off if I intend to listen to the radio, or I'll just fill up the recording capacity with music, news and commercials. He gives me a few minutes of instruction on where the various switches are and tells me how lucky I am to have someone like Suzi caring for me so much. I don't want to disillusion him with my suspicion that her main concern might really be about data collection for more precise billing purposes.

I'm glad to see everyone's got something to work on. My drunk driving case is over and Indovine grabbed the Suburban case back from me, so if nothing new comes along soon, I'm on vacation. I haven't been to the San Fernando Valley in quite a while and since it's only a half hour away, I'm taking a ride on north the 405 Freeway, over the Sepulveda Pass, to visit Stuart in Van Nuys and see how his used car business is coming along.

When I get to his warehouse he spots my yellow Hummer and comes outside to greet me with that strong handshake of his. I look around but don't see any cars. "Stuart, I thought you were going to be selling used cars here. Where are they?"

"Peter, I've developed a unique system for the selling of pre-owned vehicles. The first six cars were trucked out here, and my creative advertising sold them immediately. When the customers started asking about specific models, I talked to the people at I.R.S. to inquire about a greater selection. They told me that car theft in the five Northeast states they cover is in epidemic proportions, and if my customers aren't too fussy about color, we can be provided with practically anything they want."

"So what are you saying, you take orders for specific models now?"

"You got it, pal. You just tell me what make you want, and I can get it for you. The most popular are Camrys, Accords, and Altimas, so I've sort of become a specialist in those. I've got a couple of dealers here that are always looking to add some low-mileage ones to their front line, as long as there's no rust damage... you gotta be careful of that with East

Coast cars. You know, the snow, road salt, stuff like that."

I offer to take Stuart to lunch but he declines the invitation because he's waiting for a truckload of cars to be delivered. Just then, a large diesel car-carrier pulls up to his warehouse and honks the horn. It's got five vehicles on it with one empty slot, which means that another car must have been dropped off somewhere on the way here. The driver lowers two portable metal ramps so the cars can be driven off the truck and into Stuart's warehouse, where he'll have them cleaned up and thoroughly detailed inside and out, including the engine.

Stuart is all smiles. He proudly tells me that four of these five cars are already sold. I see that they still have New York and New Jersey license plates, but Stuart assures me that the paperwork accompanying each car must be all in order because his customers have no problem at our Department of Motor Vehicles when they go in to re-register each car, get a new California license plate and 'pink slip,' the California DMV nickname used for a document indicating that the holder has clear ownership. He claims that the paperwork that comes from back east all goes through local DMV offices perfectly.

It looks like Stuart has everything under control. My cell phone rings. It's Jack Bibberman calling. He has statements from the employees at the car dealership. I forgot to tell him that the case was taken away from me, but that's not his fault. I'll pay him for his time spent and try to get reimbursed by Indovine.

Witness statements from the dealership all seem to be in order. Before the explosions, each Suburban was brought in and first seen by a 'write-up' service manager, who then assigned each vehicle to the crew that does warranty service. Because all the Suburbans involved were recently purchased, everything done to them was covered by their factory warranties. Joe Morgan is the warranty service manager and he worked on all three of them, as well as about twelve other Suburbans during that same period of time. None of the others exploded. Being as thorough as ever, Jack also got copies of the service records on the other twelve cars. They showed the original dates of sale, mileage, and every time they came into the dealership for service. Not a one of the other twelve or the three that exploded were ever serviced anywhere else but right there at that dealership, the place where they were all purchased.

Approaching the marina I experience a Kodak moment. Slowly riding down the small access road where the boats are parked is a sight to behold. Suzi's electric cart is filled with the kid, Vinnie, the huge dog, and Olive behind the wheel. I see that in addition to running our firm, studying to be a skipper and teaching law, Suzi has also now become a driving instructor.

I park and watch this for a few minutes. When I was a kid in Chicago, my father, like all the other fathers in the city, took me out on Sunday mornings to the empty parking lot at Soldier's Field. It was tremendously large, having been designed for a stadium that could hold almost one hundred thousand people. When the Chicago Bears weren't playing, the parking lot was an ideal place to learn how to drive. The traffic in the parking lot was pretty light – but dangerous, because all the other cars were also being driven by kids being shouted at by their fathers.

Olive's father wasn't around to give her lessons, so instead of a huge parking lot she wound up with a huge dog. Vinnie's zombie-like expression tells me that he's on the verge of being in shock, but he really has nothing to worry about. The kid has everything under control as they zigzag down the road, stopping to back up and park every time they pass an empty space. If they've been doing this for the past hour or so I'm sure the driving lesson will end soon, because that cart of hers will need recharging – and I need something to eat.

Once the driving lesson is over, Vinnie tells me that next will be a real car, one of Stuart's cars - as long as no customer is coming to inspect it. Olive then surprises me. "Mister Sharp, I want to thank you very much. Suzi tells me that when I can do okay with Stuart's Town Car, you'll let me try your Hummer, because it's the closest thing we can find to the size of the armored truck."

Is she kidding? Does she think she's going to drive my beautiful yellow Hummer? No way. She'll never get behind the wheel of it. I sense something warm on the side of my face. It's the kid glaring at me. I get the message. "Okay, Olive, but first, let's see how you do with the Camry."

Olive reminds me about the upcoming Presidential parade next month and says that I should really try to get a good place to watch it from, because they've got a car in it just like mine that is painted red, white and blue. I really don't think she can tell one car from another, because she mentioned using Stuart's Town Car, and to the best of my knowledge he doesn't own one. When I call her aside to ask her about it, she tells me it's hush-hush, and that Vinnie does some work on it once in a while – that's when she'll try to drive it.

There's a knock on the hull. It's Jack B. asking to come aboard. We leave the Nascar team and go onto the aft deck to watch the sunset and discuss whatever's on his mind.

"What's up, Jack?"

"I've got some troubling information. I know you didn't authorize me to do this, but I had a strong feeling that if anyone knows how those cars exploded, it would have to be the Warranty Service Manager, Joe Morgan – so I tailed him for the past two days."

"That's pretty ambitious, Jack. Did you come up with anything?"

He looks down at the deck and hesitates for a minute. I can tell that he's bothered about something. "Come on, Jack, spit it out. What did you find out?"

He hesitates. "Well, it probably doesn't mean anything. I mean, I hate to get into this stuff, because there's enough prejudice going around. I mean…"

"Jack, either you're going to tell me, or you're not. Please make up you mind."

"Okay Pete, Joe Morgan went to a mosque. He goes there quite often to pray. His Muslim name is Yousef Mohammed."

This certainly is interesting, but I don't know what it could possibly have to do with this case.

"Jack, are you trying to tell me that you think this should mean something to us?"

"That's why I was hesitating to tell you. Just because the guy's a Muslim doesn't mean he's guilty of anything. I don't like this sort of stuff. Can we just go on with the investigation like I never learned about his religion?"

"You're right, Jack. He is just another guy until we find out otherwise… but I'm glad you told me about this. I'll just file it away in case anything else comes up. Do you know anything more about him?"

"Yeah, I was going to tell you. He's a former Navy Seal, with an extensive background in explosives."

"How did you find this out, Jack?"

"I noticed a clean spot on the wall of his service bay at the dealership. When I asked around to find out what was hanging there, one of the janitors told me that it was a picture of him with some of his Seal buddies."

This is no good. It doesn't make sense or answer any questions, but it's still no good. I check over the three cars that exploded, but don't see a name anywhere that sounds Jewish. I feel bad even looking for something like this, but it's too big an item to overlook, especially now that I know he removed the picture that identifies him as a former Seal.

Without even thinking about it, I'm looking for motive. If the vehicle drivers weren't Jewish, would a radical Islamic militant try to hurt three women just because they didn't wear black shawls or because they drive expensive big American cars? I don't think so. If he's any kind of terrorist, he's not likely to be working at the 'retail' level by trying to take out one infidel at a time. Their usual tactic is to go for large amounts of casualties in a crowded place. The combination of his religion and military background is just too much for me to put out of my mind. I tell Jack to poke around and see if he can find out when Joe took his last vacation and if he has a passport. I'm secretly hoping that he hasn't been out of the country for the past couple of years. That way, I can at least be sure that he hasn't been to one of Osama bin Laden's Mid East summer camps.

5

The next couple of days go by with nothing exciting happening. Thank goodness there are no more exploding Suburbans. Jack's been keeping his eye on Joe Morgan, and reports that he's still working every day and going to the mosque every evening. I sure hope he's not involved in this mess, because that would be very bad for Uniman Insurance.

I call a secretary who befriended me during my visits to Indovine's offices last year and she tells me that the firm purchased a brand new Suburban and had it taken apart, piece-by-piece. They didn't find anything that would cause an explosion. It probably cost Uniman Insurance about a hundred thousand for the vehicle and the experts to find out that useless information. Could they have really thought that Suburbans explode because of a design defect? Not likely. This was the deliberate work of some person who had the opportunity and the motive. I just can't figure out how any one person could have a motive to harm all three of those drivers. I call Jack B. and tell him to start concentrating on the owners of those three exploding Suburbans. Maybe there's a connection between them that could make some sense out of this whole mess.

Our boat is now a center for driving and law studies. Vinnie and Olive are here every day practicing their driving. Stuart also comes by for tutoring on his law curriculum. Suzi is the center of their world. She's finally gotten Olive trained good enough to let her drive Stuart's car. They're all hoping she does a good job, because at this point Stuart still isn't aware of the fact that she's just now learning how to drive.

They all decide to have some ice cream, and because the kid says that there's none on the boat, Vinnie and Olive take Stuart's keys so that they can drive to the market for us. This must be a plan that the kid cooked up, because I know for a fact that our freezer is full of ice cream. I watch as Vinnie and Olive walk away. When they get to the car Olive gets behind the wheel and they slowly drive off.

It's been over an hour and they still haven't come back. Stuart is not taking this very well. Suzi is not talking. That's not so unusual, because she never talks to me anyway. Jack B. is still on the boat, so he offers Stuart a ride home, offering to also drive by the market. Everyone decides to give them another hour before calling the police. I don't know what they'd tell the police. I don't think Stuart would want to report the car stolen because that would only get Olive and Vinnie in trouble... and you're not supposed to report people missing until they've been gone for at least twenty-four hours. There must be some reason why they haven't returned yet.

In the past they've been known to hop in the back of the armored truck for a quickie, but they're not likely to do that this evening... not with Stuart waiting for his Camry - and some ice cream.

Finally, at just a few minutes to ten, the phone rings. It's Vinnie. When I say his name into the phone, everyone shouts out at me "Are they okay? Was there an accident?"

I smile as I put the phone down and make the announcement. "Oh no, nothing unusual. They're both fine. They're in jail."

Strange as it sounds, we're all relieved. There's a general good feeling going around the room. No accident, no injuries, just jail... and as far as Vinnie is concerned, this is quite normal, because it's happened so many time in the past.

Stuart suddenly comes out of the ether. "What the hell are they doing in jail?"

"I don't know Stu, but if you and Jack want to go over to the L.A.P.D.'s Pacific Division on Culver and Centinela, I'm sure either the desk sergeant or Vinnie will explain it to you."

They get into Jack Bibberman's old junk and head over to the jail. I make sure to let them know that I'm turning off my phone and going to bed. Whatever it is can wait until tomorrow. I'm closed for the night – which is too bad, because as usual, anything that Vinnie gets involved in is a tremendously interesting adventure. Some day they're going to make a movie about his life story. The only problem is that I don't think anyone will believe it.

The next morning Stuart calls to explain what happened the night before - and to ask a small favor. He tells me it's partly his fault that Vinnie and Olive got arrested. Stuart wanted to surprise Vinnie and his new wife with a present. He knew they both liked the George C. Scott movie '*Patton*,' so he bought them each a pearl-handled forty-five caliber automatic Patton-style handgun to wear while driving the armored cars. Stuart hid both guns and holsters in his car's glove compartment.

When Olive was driving to the market, she mis-judged the distance between the Camry and a Police squad car that was parked in the market's lot. There were two cops in the car having coffee and donuts, with several other police cars nearby, all on a coffee break.

It was a big surprise when Olive slammed into the L.A.P.D. black-and-white, completely wiping out the front end of Stuart's Camry and shaking the cops up in their car. Coffee and donuts went flying all over their front seat and dashboard.

All the other cops ran over to both cars to see if everyone was okay. When things calmed down, they got around to asking Olive for her drivers license and registration. While Olive, an as of yet unlicensed driver, was stuttering a feeble excuse, another cop walked around to the passenger side, shined his flashlight into the car, and asked Vinnie to open the glove compartment to get the registration info.

When Vinnie followed the cop's request, the two shiny new automatics popped out onto his lap.

If there's anything that cops don't like to see in run-of-the-mill traffic stops, it's guns.

In a matter of seconds there were at least a half-dozen guns pointing at both Olive and Vinnie until they each exited their car, hands in the air. They were then handcuffed and taken to the police station to be detained for a number of charges, including suspicion of grand theft auto, unauthorized possession of weapons, and some vehicle code sections relating to reckless driving and endangerment.

When Stuart arrived at the station he convinced the police that the car wasn't stolen. He also was able to explain away the gun charges by having them check their computers and verify that he operated an armored truck service.

Vinnie and Olive were finally released from police custody, but the car was placed in the official automobile impound lot – and that's the favor Stuart is asking. He wants me to please go to the lot and have the car towed over to his warehouse so it can be checked out to see if repairs are possible.

Stuart's done a lot for me in the past, so if it's at all possible, I always try to help him out.

The Police Impound lot is in a terrible neighborhood populated by auto junkyards, car repair places, a plating factory and several other poorly maintained industrial buildings made out of sheet metal. To make matters worse, the street has potholes big enough to swim in, and this Hummer was not designed to give a soft luxury ride.

Before entering the lot you must get past a surly gate attendant sitting behind a one-inch thick plate glass window near the front door. I guess there are plenty of irate people who come to get their car returned after it's been towed away because it was left alone 'for just a minute' in some unauthorized place – like a handicapped only parking space, in front of a fire hydrant, or other spot where people who don't give a damn about anyone but themselves decide to leave a vehicle.

This particular attendant looks familiar, like I've seen him on television somewhere. He's got long scraggly hair, a rough complexion, bad teeth, a tattoo on his neck, and a cigarette hanging out of his mouth. If I've seen him somewhere before it was probably on a reality show like *Cops*, as one of the many skinny drunk guys without shirts on, who always seem to be getting arrested for beating their wives.

After identifying myself to this *Cops* star, he grants me permission to see Stuart's vehicle if I'll pay for the charges to date. After charging my credit card for the tow plus two days' storage, he tells me that the keys are in the glove compartment and directs me to where it's parked. The tow truck backed it up against the lot's concrete retaining wall, where it now sits waiting for me. I delicately walk past the growling German shepherd chained to the wall and enter the outdoor part of the yard. Following some advice another dog owner once told me, I don't smile at the guard dog. They consider the showing of teeth as an aggressive act.

The Camry doesn't look like it's in a drivable condition, so I call a friend of mine who operates a tow truck in the Marina and tell him to meet me at the impound lot. Not surprisingly, he knows exactly where the place is. I go into the glove box to retrieve the keys, because you must turn the ignition on in order to remove the vehicle from the 'park' gear position. When reaching into the glove box, my hand inadvertently brushes against the remote trunk lid release and I hear the trunk pop open. No problem. I slam the glove box shut, and walking around to the rear of the car, to close the trunk, I see that something large in the there, like a great big sack of laundry. Upon closer inspection I see that it's really a bed sheet wrapped around something. When I push it over to see what's inside, a hand flops out. It's a dead body.

6

This is not an accessory that automobile manufacturers usually include with a vehicle, so I assume it's a special New Jersey dealer-installed option.

At this point, I think the worst thing to do is bring the police into it, because the body was probably delivered from back east with the car, so it's not a California case. I've helped out the local authorities on past occasions, so I don't see any reason why I shouldn't help out the New Jersey cops with a case.

Fortunately, my friend Victor Gutierrez has what they call a 'vanity' phone number that's so easy to remember, I don't have to write it down. I pick up my cell phone and call him at '1800AUTOPSY.'

When the tow truck arrives, I tell him that the delivery point has been changed. Instead of Stuart's place in Van Nuys, this car is going to Victor's place, out near Pasadena. I then call Stuart and tell him to meet me at Victor's.

Stuart and I both arrive at Victor's before the tow truck, so I've got a few minutes to explain to him what I found in the trunk of his car. There's no need for him to claim that he had nothing to do with the body being put in the trunk because I have no doubt that he's not connected with it in any way.

54

When the tow truck arrives, Victor comes outside to take a look at his latest client. After the tow truck leaves, Victor opens the trunk and spends less than a minute looking at the merchandise.

"Peter, I'm going to save you a couple of thousand dollars on an autopsy. Your passenger here has a bullet hole in the center of his head."

I thank Victor for the quick diagnosis, and assign him the task of a partial exam to determine the estimated time of death and anything else we can use to identify the body, like fingerprints, dental records, or whatever he can learn. I tell him to prepare a sheet on the corpse, with a photo, and enough info to send to Philly's missing persons department.

It only took Victor a day to finish his assignment and he mailed me the bullet, photo, and other descriptive information. He didn't do an autopsy, but if the body was brought out to California by truck, he estimates the probable time of death to be at least ten days prior to Stuart's accepting delivery of the car. That's the information I really wanted to have, in case some idiot cop thinks Stuart might be involved in the murder. I tell Victor to leave the car in his garage – the police will probably be coming for it later this week.

Now it's time for a hypothetical telephone conversation, so I bravely call my ex-wife Myra, our County's newly elected District Attorney. The people in her office all know who I am and how I helped her get elected, so my call gets put through.

"Hello Peter. Listen, I've got a lot of things to do today, so I hope this isn't a social call."

"Myra honey, that ship's already sailed. I've got a hypothetical question to ask you. What if a person orders a large item from out of state – something like a piece of furniture, like an armoire, and when it gets delivered she opens it up to find a dead body. Would she be in any trouble?"

"I already told you I was busy today Peter, so let's cut the crap. Which one of your idiot friends got stuck with a body? No, never mind… it has to be either Jack, Stuart or Vinnie, and I'd guess that the body's already at Victor's place, right? Okay. Your silence is enough of an answer. I'll send a team out there to get it. And Peter…"

"Yes my dear?"

"Make sure that whichever of the three stooges is involved in this farce stays in town for a while, because we'll have to get a full statement."

She always did have the ability to see right through me. I tell her she's right about it being at Victor's place, but don't give her any more information, hiding behind the attorney-client privilege. She isn't too happy with that, but must be just too busy to argue with me. I guess those exploding Suburban cases are giving her some problems. I'm glad Indovine took that one back, because it looks like it turned into a real hot potato.

I've got some far out theories on the exploding Suburbans cases, but extensive investigation will probably be involved and my office would never authorize an expense like that on a case we don't have anymore. I figure that Indovine will jump at the chance to spend some of Uniman's money, so I call his office. I must be an important person, because this is the second time today that I call a big shot and get put right through.

"Indovine here, what do you want Sharp?"

I would have felt a lot more confident if he would have used my first name, but he took the call, and that's the important thing.

"Charles, I want to do some investigation on your Suburban class action case, and it's going to cost some money. I'd like your authorization."

"Sharp, you're no longer on that case. Our class action department has it, and they're quite capable of doing their own investigation."

"Okay Charles. I know you're a busy guy, so I'll only say this once. Last time we had a discussion like this, you also turned me down. And if you remember, I wound up saving your client over a million bucks and at the same time made a schmuck out of you... which isn't too hard to do when you pull one of your arrogant acts. Now listen to me. If I can show that the class action has no merit whatsoever, it'll save your client a multi-million dollar settlement, and my investigation will cost a lot less than those assholes in your class action department wasted in buying and tearing apart that brand new Suburban. Furthermore, I'll give you my word that if I save your client's ass again this time, I'll make it look like it was all your idea. Now all you have to do is say yes or no. I'm going to do the investigation anyway, and whoever's dime it's on will get all the credit. Do we have a deal?"

After a few seconds of silence, I get what I expected – a grumbling acceptance.

With Indovine now paying for the investigation I might be able to kill a couple of birds with one stone, one of which being the answers behind the I.R.S. company that sells cars to Stuart. If nothing else, they certainly are generous. No other dealer I'm aware of would include a free dead body with the purchase of a car.

To keep things going smoothly, I advise Stuart to not say anything to his New 'Joisy' supplier, and to keep ordering vehicles as if nothing happened. Once Myra gets that body from Victor, I'll make some deal with her to try and keep it out of the papers so that the New Jersey car company won't know that an investigation is going on out here. I warn Stuart that on all future deliveries, he must make sure that each trunk is open and inspected before he accepts a vehicle. If another body turns up, we want it to be the car-carrier company who gets stuck with it before the car gets driven into Stuart's garage.

While I'm on the phone giving Stuart all his instructions, he lets me know that Vinnie and Olive finally confessed to the fact that Olive didn't know how to drive when she accepted the armored truck job from him. He was still feeling guilty about those guns in the glove box that caused their arrest, so he accepted her apology and enrolled her in a real driving school. Maybe now I'm off the hook for promising to let her drive my Hummer.

Also following my advice, Stuart doesn't tell the dynamic duo that they were driving around with a dead body in the trunk. Olive had a bad experience with a cadaver being delivered to Victor's place last year, and I don't want to see her upset like that again. Stuart begs out of the conversation because another load of six cars is being delivered, and he intends to videotape the opening and inspection of each trunk.

Jack B. came up with some new info about Joe Morgan. His bank account shows some deposits that exceed his salary at the dealership. Too many coincidences are popping up here. I hope that no one else starts connecting the dots, because it looks like Joe Morgan may be heading for a fall.

It's time that I found out more about the New Jersey company where Stuart gets his cars. Now that Indovine will be reimbursing our expenses, I send Jack B. to New Jersey. His assignment is to pretend like he owns a used car dealership in the San Fernando Valley and was referred to them by Stuart. I've already prepped Stuart to back up Jack's cover story.

Jack calls from the east coast to let me know that the car company returned his phone call and he will be meeting with a guy named Billy tomorrow afternoon. I tell him to check with New Jersey's Motor Vehicle Records Department to try and locate the previous owners of the cars that Stuart purchased

– especially the one in which the body was found. If he can get to interview an owner or two, he's to find out the details about their cars: when they were stolen, who the insurance companies involved are, when they were paid off, and which police precinct they made their stolen vehicle report to.

I want to see if there are any inconsistencies in the chain of information. A timeline is involved, and if anything is out of place, it should stick out like a sore thumb. Each owner should have made a stolen car report within twenty-four hours of the theft and they should also have collected their policy benefits from the insurance company thirty days later. After the insurance company recovers the cars, they should have records of sales to I.R.S., and if Stuart is the final customer, he should get the car no sooner than two weeks later – and that's if everything is done as efficiently as possible. If any step along the way occurs before or after it's supposed to, I'll catch it.

There's plenty of action going on, but I'm not getting paid for any of it. Fortunately for my bank account, the kid's Marina clientele is still active. Her stepfather was retained to represent the apartment building and slip owners in their actions against non-paying tenants. There are thousands of apartment and boat slip tenants, so legal action is usually required on a steady basis. The most common problem that occurs is when the owner of an old boat decides that he doesn't want it anymore – usually about a year or so after its engine freezes up. They get tired of paying several hundred dollars a month slip rental for a junk boat that doesn't even run, so they abandon it.

The landlords have provisions in their slip rental agreements giving them the right to auction off any abandoned boat after judgment is obtained against the owner for non-payment of slip rent. The legal work is almost identical on every case. All Suzi has to do is change the name of the boat, the name of the defendant, the dates, and the amounts. The cases get filed with the court by mail, and the papers are sent out for service with either Jack Bibberman or the Marshal's office. The only thing that an attorney like me is needed for is to provide a name and a State Bar membership number in the upper left hand corner of the complaints that get filed.

I don't have to do much other than front the kid's law practice. It doesn't pay a hell of a lot, but the Marina lets us park our boat in the slip and pays a minimum retainer, so we'll always have a place to live.

Jack checks in from New Jersey. He's done everything I asked him to do and he's returning late this afternoon, so I make arrangements to have him picked up at the airport. Olive has her learner's permit and she's desperate for places to drive, so she and Vinnie will be at LAX when Jack's plane lands. I'm looking forward to getting his reports, so they'll all be stopping by for dinner on their way back from the airport. Stuart must have gotten a tip from the kid that the Asian boys are bringing Chinese food over tonight, so he'll be here too... about the same time that the food gets delivered. Suzi's already made arrangements for plenty of extra portions to be included in the delivery.

While the Asian boys are spreading out the food, we're all spreading out Jack's reports. The boat's a hub of activity, with ten people aboard. The dog is watching dog food commercials on television. Suzi grabs the remote and turns up the volume because she sees Myra on the screen.

The reporter is interviewing her about an arrest that was made of a suspect in the double homicide caused by that exploding Suburban. It's Joe Morgan. I knew he was going to get busted sooner or later, but I didn't think it would be this soon.

Myra was asked about any information they may have learned from Morgan as to his motive. Her answer was a surprise to all of us. "We haven't interrogated Mister Morgan because he has counsel - the law firm of Charles Indovine, the same firm that represents the dealership where Mister Morgan is employed. They have informed this office that we are not to question him until his attorney is present. They intend to assign this criminal case to an associate of theirs, attorney Peter Sharp, who I'm sure you all know is familiar to this office."

It looks like I'm back in business. I had a hunch that Morgan was involved, but I didn't think that Myra would go after him just because he's a Muslim. I can't imagine what else she has on him, but I'm sure I'll find out soon enough. Rather than break protocol by calling her at home this evening, I think it best to meet at her office tomorrow morning. I want to play this one strictly by the book, because it may turn into a high-profile case.

This meeting is the first one I've had here on a case since Myra got elected. I don't know how much she knows, so instead of trying to convince her that my client is innocent, I decide to let her talk. A long time ago I was told that you can't learn anything while you're talking – only when you're listening. Besides, I haven't even had a chance to interview my client.

Indovine called first thing this morning, assigned the case to me, and messengered over a retainer check for over ten thousand dollars, which is just the beginning on a case that might lead to the prosecutor going for the death penalty. Before the call got to me, the kid let him know about the investigation expenses, so that was added to the check too.

Myra explains to me that Morgan was arrested for the usual reasons – motive, means, and opportunity, along with the fact that they found explosive devices in his house.

I already knew about his capability and opportunity, but was curious as to what she considered to be his motive for these crimes.

Myra explains that two of the owners of the vehicles have been customers at the dealership for over twenty years. During that period of time they were always bringing their cars in for service, and if there was a decision to be made as to whether or not a repair is covered by the factory warranty, it was always made by Joe Morgan.

The owners admitted to a long-running scheme of bribing Morgan to make decisions to have the warranty cover many unauthorized repairs. After the successful prosecution of a warranty service manager in Orange County for running the same scheme, the car owners got scared and told Morgan they didn't want any part of the plan – and that they'd pay for their repairs, rather then go to jail.

The prosecution's argument on motive is that Morgan wanted to scare them into realizing that they should keep on paying for him to authorize repairs. Each owner has agreed to testify.

"Okay, I can see where you've got something to hang your hat on for the first two non-lethal explosions, but how's your office planning to tie in the third explosion - the one that killed the two women? That vehicle was owned by the dealership, not the general manager. He didn't have to pay for repairs, so he couldn't have been involved in a bribery scheme with my client."

Myra admits that I have a point there, but she promises that her office is working on another angle with the general manager – some other reason why Morgan wanted to scare him too.

"Fine, but if you admit that all he wanted to do is scare these people, then I won't expect you to be looking to stick a needle in his arm."

She tells me that the results of the investigation aren't in yet, so no decision has been made on whether they'll be going for the death penalty.

I have only one more question to ask her, and I think I already know the answer to it. "Just one more thing, Myra, what turned you on to Morgan in the first place?"

She tells me that they received an anonymous tip from an informant. Just what I thought. Criminal defense attorneys have been dealing with the prosecution's confidential informants and anonymous tipsters since the judicial system was created. Judges are very cooperative with prosecutors, so defense attorneys find it almost impossible to discover the identity of a confidential informant. Actually, that might be a good thing, but we all know that it's terribly misused too often. There are countless times when police don't really have good enough probable cause to break in somewhere, so they might 'drop their own dime' and phone in an anonymous tip that they then get to act upon.

Confidential informants are usually criminals who've made some deal with the prosecution to get their own cases or sentences reduced in some way, so they're not that reliable. Too many stories about lying jailhouse snitches have been exposed. True, there's the rare undercover police agent who must be protected, but it's too rare to consider.

I think that this case falls into the category of misdirection - a type of case where the real culprit makes an anonymous tip to lead the authorities away from him and instead to a more convenient suspect who the police can then hang a case on. But it doesn't make any difference now, other than to confirm a theory of mine. I did get some information out of her today, but most of it was the bad news. The good news isn't what she told me – it was what she didn't tell me. Her office obviously has no idea that Joe is a Muslim.

I've got a lot of questions to ask my new criminal client, so while I'm downtown I might as well stop in to say hello.

The County's new twin tower facility is not a fun place to visit. When Joe Morgan is brought into the attorney interview room I introduce myself and we sit down to go over some of the things that Myra told me.

After about a half hour of conversation, I come to the conclusion that this guy did not plant those bombs and had no intention of killing anyone. It's rare to find an innocent criminal client, but when you do, they're not too difficult to spot.

We discuss the bribe accusation, and he readily admits to it, but claims that when those two owners decided to stop paying, he was happy with their decision. It had been going on long enough, and he felt that pushing it any further might result in his getting caught and the loss of his job. Evidently there's some bad blood between the dealership's general manager and his assistant, and if the assistant gets fired, Joe thought he might have been in line for a promotion.

This conflicts with what I was told, but I haven't had a chance to talk to those owners yet, and I'm sure that their feelings about Joe wanting to scare them were merely the result of aggressive questioning by the D.A.'s investigator. Once I get them on the witness stand, I'm sure they'll fold like a deck of cards.

Another thing that I'm curious about is why he removed that picture from the wall in his service bay.

"Mister Sharp, everyone knows I was a Navy Seal. I'm proud of it. It's just that after those first two Suburbans exploded, I figured that it wouldn't be too smart to advertise the fact that I was trained in how to use explosives, so I took the picture down in case some strangers came snooping around."

I'm convinced he's innocent of the murder charge. I keep going over the facts All the way back to the Marina, but all I can see him guilty of is some larceny of the manufacturer's money by authorizing warranty repairs to those owners' vehicles over the years – certainly not murder or trying to scare anyone.

The explosive devices they found in his house were some things he claims to have been putting together for a fourth of July fireworks display, not to murder someone. The matter of his religion didn't come up in the conversation. He didn't ask me about

67

my religious preference, so I didn't ask him about his.

The District Attorney didn't go for a grand jury indictment in Joe's case, so he'll be arraigned in the municipal court next week and a date will be set for his preliminary hearing.

In most cases, time is a criminal defense's ally, because there's always the possibility that prosecution witnesses will be hard to locate and forget things. In this case, Joe agrees that we shouldn't waive any time. The prosecution doesn't have that strong of a case and we don't want to give them a lot of time to try and make it stronger.

Back at the boat, I make out a full report for Indovine's office. He tells me that I shouldn't spare any expense on this case, because clearing Morgan will also be clearing the dealership. That'll leave only the automobile manufacturer holding the bag for any design defect, and since Uniman is his client, and not the manufacturer, Indovine doesn't care what happens to GM.

They still don't get it. They probably will never get it. This may only become a class action because two law firms want it to be a class action. The legal fees for a class action plaintiff's firm can be astronomical, and the defense will also wind up with seven figures by the time it's all over. This part of the system stinks - and I'm a part of it - a sworn officer of the court. It makes me sick to see the way some of these firms play the system like a jukebox. But who am I to complain? I've already accepted a ten thousand dollar retainer, and if this case goes to trial, my fee will probably be more than five times that amount. I guess I'm no different than the rest of them; I take the money and keep my mouth shut. But if everything goes okay, sometimes I try to minimize the large amounts that the others try to extort out of the system and their deep pocket clients.

Olive's Court appearance is coming up soon and Stuart has asked me to handle it. She's still facing charges for driving without a license when she drove into that police car in the market's parking lot. I go to the courthouse, and to my unpleasant surprise, the deputy city attorney is the same one I dealt with on the federal agent's drunk driving charge; Miss Seymour. She's as happy to see me as I am to see her. Our conversation is not exactly cordial, but she agrees to go into the judge's chambers with me to discuss the case. The only reason she'd like to dispose of it is because she knows that if it goes to trial I'll be sending out subpoenas to every one of the cops there that night, and that will take at least seven or eight peace officers off the street and cost the City a lot of overtime that they can't afford.

We're buzzed into chambers. It's Judge Parker, and he remembers me.

"What can I do for you today Mister Sharp? Are you looking for a dismissal, with a five thousand dollar court cost? You know, we call that bribery around here."

Good. He's got a sense of humor. Unfortunately I'm the butt of it, but I can work with that. I've got a lot to do in preparation for Joe Morgan's preliminary hearing, so I decide to try and wrap this thing up right here and now.

"Your Honor, I don't think they've got a case here." This brings the Deputy City Attorney to her feet, loudly protesting. The judge knows that I must have something in mind, because he remembers I'm a clever dealmaker. He waives off the prosecutor's argument and signals for her to sit down and for me to continue.

"First, we all know how much time it will take for all those police officers to be brought in off the street. They include members of the Los Angeles Police Department, Los Angeles Sheriffs, Culver City Police, and California Highway Patrol. It'll be one pain in the rear for them all to get served and brought in here.

"Added to that, the entire incident took place in the market's parking lot, on private property, and not on the public street.

"Furthermore, the car entered the parking lot almost two hundred yards away from where the collision occurred, and not one of your officers can place her behind the wheel before the car pulled into the parking lot. For all we know, this is probably a simple case of a guy using a large parking lot on private property, at night, to give his girlfriend a driving lesson.

"And lastly, I've been authorized by the driver's employer to offer full restitution to the City for all repairs to the damaged squad car. If we can make a deal to plead no contest to this charge, and allow for a retroactive expunging of the record upon her showing proof of a valid driver's license, I'd like to wrap this thing up today and prepare for a murder case I'm working on."

No comment from the prosecutor. Judge Parker breaks the silence. "If the City Attorney's office will go along with it, it's okay with me. Mister Sharp, you've raised some good points here today and the offer of full reimbursement to the City and no need to bring in a lot of cops off the street works for me."

The deal is made and I'm on my way back to the boat, where my clients are anxiously waiting for me to return. I'm sure for the next couple of years Olive will be paying Stuart every week for the damage she caused to both Stuart's Camry and the squad car, but that's the way the ball bounces. If you can't do the time, don't do the crime.

Back at the boat, the crew is sitting in the salon watching the dog watch television. I explain to Olive that her case is over, but that Stuart will be getting a nice big bill from the City for squad car repairs. They all want to know how the deal works with my entering a plea that gets expunged in the future.

1203.4 (a) is one of the few sections of the California Penal Code that's so self-explanatory, even this group gathered in front of me could probably read and understand it. But, just to make sure, I paraphrase it for them, adding a little history that doesn't appear in the law books.

"The section of the law that covers expungement of records stems from back in the early 1960's, when a taxicab driver got into a dispute with Mrs. Sterling, his female passenger. They were arguing about her payment of the fare. The cab driver wasn't going to let her get away with what he considered was wrongful conduct, so he made a citizen's arrest and turned her over to the police.

"The wheels of justice ground at their regular slow speed and eventually, all the misdemeanor charges against Ms. Sterling were dismissed... but she wasn't through yet. She brought suit against the cab company for being imprisoned by the driver and wrongfully prosecuted – and she won against them in civil court. But was that enough for her? Noooo... that wasn't all... she then sued the City of Oakland, where everything took place. She wanted them to destroy her fingerprints and booking photo, claiming that even though she was never convicted of a crime, the mere fact that she was in their criminal record system might hurt her some time in the future.

"As a result of the efforts of Mrs. Sterling and quite a few other people over the years, California and a number of other jurisdictions have enacted laws allowing for people who have convictions for certain minor crimes against them to finish up with whatever conditions the court orders and then have an opportunity to have their plea or conviction reversed, a dismissal entered, and the records expunged. And that's what will happen for Olive. On her behalf, I

made a deal with the judge that if she finishes her
driver's education and reimburses the City for
damages to their squad car, her plea of No Contest
will be withdrawn, a plea of not guilty will be
retroactively entered, and the case will be dismissed."

They give me a round of light applause. I
bow, accept their adulation, and remind them that the
fee I'm now owed for that brilliant legal work and
lecture is their full cooperation in going over all the
reports that Jack brought back from New York. In no
time at all, the entire parquet floor of the boat's salon
is covered with paper and everyone's going over
every word.

After what seems like hours, we get
everything gathered up off the floor and put into
order. Stuart brought some file folders with him that
are especially designed for car dealers to keep track
of the expenses incurred on a vehicle from its
acquisition to its sale. The folders are like big
envelopes open at the top. Outside of the folders are
places to enter amounts spent and things done in
order to get the car sold.

When we're done, we have everything back
in order. The cars were stolen. Timely reports were
made to the police. The policyholders got paid for
their losses. The cars were recovered and sold to
I.R.S., who then re-sold them to Stuart and shipped
them by truck to Van Nuys, California. Every 'i' was
dotted and 't' was crossed. Perfect record keeping
and compliance on every car.

As far as everyone's concerned, it's a legit operation from start to finish. Stuart is happy. Somewhere in the back of my mind, I'm still not satisfied. It's just too neat a package. Something has to be wrong somewhere, because this deal is still too good to be true.

Myra calls. The caller ID on my display shows that she's calling from home.

"Hi, kid, what's up? You ready to dismiss the murder charges against my client, wanna get laid, or both?"

"None of the above. I called because I'm worried about the motive. You may have been right when you were in my office. I can't connect him to the general manager's explosion. You want to talk deal here?"

"I know what he did, and I know what he didn't do, and you're gonna have to believe me when I tell you that he didn't do any of the things you're charging him with. I admit he may have been involved in some hanky-panky with those first two owners, but unless you want to amend your complaint to larceny for taking those bribes, then we don't have much to talk about."

"I can't do that Pete. This is the first major case the office has had since I got elected to this job, and I don't want to fall flat on my face."

"I agree with you hon, but I can't allow my client to take a dive to help your image. Maybe we can work something else out that everyone's happy with."

"Okay, I'll try to think of something, but there are about a million new competing budget requests. Do you have any idea of what it's going to cost Los Angeles County when the President comes to town? Everyone working overtime, background investigations…"

"What does that have to do with you? The District Attorney's office has nothing to do with visits by politicians."

"Yeah, but all the money we spend during those visits has to come from somewhere, and our office is a favorite target. We may have badges, but we don't have those nifty uniforms to make us look like heroes."

This was one of the longest telephone conversations I've had with Myra since before we got married, when we used to spend hours on the phone with each other. If we could have talked like this when we were married, I'd probably still be living with her in that house in Brentwood Glen. Maybe things worked out for the best. I don't have a wife anymore, but I do have a young ward and a huge Saint Bernard – and the boat of my dreams. If Myra would come to her senses she could share it all, but that's unlikely considering the bundle she inherited. She doesn't need to share anything I've got now, because she can afford to buy it outright on her own. So much for bad timing. Her wealthy grandfather passed away shortly after I got tossed out.

The only sharing I'll be doing is some wine with Laverne tonight, because until I get to meet George, she's my favorite neighbor.

Joe Morgan's preliminary hearing is set for this afternoon and I've already told him that not much is going to happen today. Like most other criminal clients, he wanted to know why we weren't going to put up a vigorous defense, so I explained that unlike a trial, all the prosecution must do at a 'prelim' is show that a crime was committed and that there is probable cause to bind the defendant over for trial. Guilt needn't be shown. The district attorney only has to show that the defendant 'probably' was involved in some way.

Defense attorneys rarely put on a case at a prelim. They just sit back and see what the prosecution's case looks like. You're allowed to cross-examine the prosecution's witnesses, but you don't want to ask too many questions, for fear of giving away whatever kind of defense you might be using when the case goes to trial.

Myra sends in one of her best deputies for Joe's prelim, and he does it right by the numbers. First, the coroner establishes that there were deaths involved and talks about the autopsy results and causes of death, due to the explosion. Next are the detectives who arrested Joe on an anonymous tip that was called in to them. They're also the ones who searched his house and found what they considered to be explosive devices – the stuff that Joe told me were for a fireworks display he was working on. I don't want to try to tear their testimony apart at this time, because it would probably be an effort in futility. I know that the next witness will be the first exploding Suburban's owner, and he'll be testifying about the bribes paid to Joe for unwarranted repairs made to his vehicles over the years.

This is a slam-dunk for the prosecution, but that's to be expected because most prelims are – and there are no surprises today because Joe gets bound over for trial in the Superior Court. As planned, we refuse to waive time and the trial is scheduled for next month. Myra's deputy tries to talk me into waiving time, but the only way I'll do it is if they'll agree to a reasonable bail amount for Joe. They won't, so no deal is made. Joe will be staying in custody until trial, and the prosecution only has another couple of weeks to finish putting together what I think is a pretty weak case.

When we get to trial I intend to call an explosive expert in who will testify that there's no way the device they found at Joe's house could ever have been configured to set off a bomb in any car.

I'll also be working over the two Suburban owners about their bribes to Joe, to find out what kind of deal was offered them for their testimony – like no filing of charges for conspiracy to commit larceny. I'll also be grilling them about their thoughts that Joe was angry that their little repair scheme was closed down.

I don't see any way they can get a conviction in this case. If Myra has the brain I think she has, she'll be offering me a deal before the trial. Joe and I discussed a plea bargain and he agrees to seriously consider one if they'll drop the murder charges and let him plead to the briberies.

Back at the boat I see that there's a crew of guys applying some tinted material to the wheelhouse windows. From the outside that tint looks too dark, but when stepping inside I see that the special tint only prevents light from entering – you can still see outside very easily. It's that special kind of tint that only affects the side that the light is on. In the daytime, you can see outside, but nobody can see in. At night, when the interior is lit up, people outside can see in, but you can't see out.

There's no sense in asking who hired them, or what this whole procedure is for, because I know that forces beyond my control are at work around here.

The phone rings and my caller ID display shows a number that looks familiar. The caller is a female.

"Hello, Mister Peter Sharp?"

There's a lot of telemarketing going on, so whenever a strange voice asks for me by my first and last name, I assume it's a stranger who wants to give me some sales pitch for something I'm definitely not interested in. Past experience has shown that if you start out by asking some questions, you can usually get the telemarketer to back off. They never want to give you their name, and will never give you a location they're calling from, or a telephone number to call them back at.

I start out with my first question. "Who's calling please?"

To my surprise it's not a telemarketer. "Mister Sharp, can I call you Peter? This is Patty Seymour."

"I'm sorry Miss Seymour, but I don't recognize your name. Is this about a current case we're both working on?"

"No, I'm the calendar deputy City Attorney in the West Los Angeles courtroom you appeared in a couple of times this month. I'm afraid we didn't get off to a very good start in our past few meetings."

Jeez. This is the ex-district attorney's niece – the one who hates my guts for getting her bi-sexual uncle ousted from office.

"Oh, yeah… listen, I really am sorry about your uncle. I had nothing personal against him, I mean, he really dressed nice and now he'll probably wind up being the governor, so everything worked out for the best. If you…"

"No, no Peter. I know it was nothing personal. I'm not calling for that at all. I'm calling to ask if you'd like to accompany me to a legal function. Judge Parker will be addressing our legal group and he suggested that I bring you along as my guest. It's a monthly meeting of our law luncheon club, and he'll be talking about confidential informants and probable cause."

This is a pleasant surprise. I really thought she hated me. I guess the only way to attract members of the opposite sex is by ignoring them. That must be true, because over the years, thousands of women have been using that system, obviously trying to attract me.

"Well yes, that would be nice. Why don't you e-mail me the information, and I'll pick you up."

If I remember correctly, she wasn't too bad to look at. This could be very interesting. I've already got a connection with the District Attorney's office, and if this relationship gives me access to the City Attorney's office, my opportunities as a criminal defense lawyer will definitely be bumped up a notch.

After hanging up with Patty, I see that the window tinting crew has gone. There's a knock on the hull - it's Tom and Lori, the married couple who are dockmasters at our anchorage. After inviting them aboard we exchange small talk about the Marina for a while and they surprise me with some news. "Mister Sharp, your little one called us earlier... we're here to give you your boat handling test. You're the only one on the dock who hasn't taken it yet. Will you be driving from down here at the lower steering station, or from up on the flybridge?"

What the hell is she up to? She knows I don't even know how to start the engines on this huge boat. I look towards her stateroom. The door is partly ajar and I see her peering out, pointing up in the air.

"Mister Sharp, did you hear us? Will you be driving from down here or up on the bridge?"

I received the signal from my coach. "Er, uh, I'll be doing it from up on the bridge."

"Very smart, Mister Sharp. That's the best place to do it from. Much better all-around vision from up there."

"Yeah, that's what I thought."

Suzi comes out tells us that she's afraid to watch, so she'll be hiding in her stateroom. This impresses Tom and Lori.

"She's such a little doll... we just love her."

The dockmasters step off of our boat and go up on the flybridge of a neighbor's boat, where they sit down and prepare to make notes on their clipboards as they view my boat handling performance. This may wind up becoming one of my most embarrassing moments.

The kid comes out of her stateroom and gives me only one instruction. "When you're up there, put your hands on the clutch controls, but don't hold on too tight. I'll be working them from down here, and I don't want to feel you fighting me from up there."

What a devil she is. The windows were tinted so that the dock masters wouldn't see her behind the wheel of the lower steering station. She's got me acting as a shill for her. Now I know how a ventriloquist's dummy feels.

It's too late to do anything about it now, so after she starts the engines I climb up the ladder to the flybridge and unsnap the control covers.

From what I've been told by some dock neighbors, at the slow speed you're moving while near the dock, the steering wheel doesn't do much. There's just not enough water passing by the rudders at the speed required to make a difference. The only things that count at that snail's pace are the gears. With a twin-engine boat, by properly shifting between forward and reverse, you should be able to make the boat completely rotate in its own length. They also tell me that the main difference between an experienced boat handler and a novice is that the old pro bumps into as many things as the amateur, but has more eloquent excuses. The beginner will simply say 'oops,' or 'sorry,' while the experienced boater will be clever enough to blame it on a slipping transmission or some other mechanical problem. He won't ever take the blame – it's the boat's fault.

I'll just have to believe what they say, because I don't think there's any way I could ever drive this thing. I feel lucky every time I succeed in getting my Hummer into its parking space.

Up on the flybridge, I place my hands on the clutch controls and notice that the dockmasters are signaling me to start. The clutch controls move into reverse, taking my hands with them, and the boat slowly starts to back out of the slip. It's a good thing nobody's up here to see the perspiration dripping from my forehead. My palms aren't too dry either. After about thirty seconds of backing out, we're clear of the slip. One of the gears stays in reverse and the other shifts into forward. The boat starts to swing around, pointing toward the channel. When it's facing the channel, the clutch in reverse shifts into forward and we start to move ahead.

We take a short trip down the channel and then stop, turn around, and head back for the slip. I look down at the slip and see that while we were out, it shrunk. It actually got smaller. There's no way this big fat boat can fit back into it.

Obviously the kid doesn't see things the way I do, which is no surprise to me. The boat gets aimed at the slip, and after some precision control moves slowly goes forward until we gracefully pull right back in to where we started. It's a perfect job of parking – no bumping into anything - nothing but slip. The dockmasters come back down from their viewing perch, pick up our dock lines and hold them for up me. I scurry down the ladder and onto the foredeck, take the dock lines they hand me and fasten them to the cleats on our boat.

The kid comes out onto the deck and asks the dock masters. "Is it over yet?"

They think this is so cute. She was so afraid that she hid below and now wants to know if it's over or not. What a little fraud she is. She plays the dockmasters like they're a slot machine… and it pays off.

"Oh, Suzi, you had nothing to be afraid of. Mister Sharp did a wonderful job of handling the boat. You should be very proud of him." As a reward for passing the Marina's boat-handling test, they hand me a gift plaque with the words 'An experienced sailor knows that the sea isn't his enemy… it's the hard stuff around the edges.' Naturally, I thank them from the bottom of my heart.

As the kid walks past me, I hear her mutter something. I don't think I want to know what it was.

It's Wednesday afternoon and as promised, my date is waiting for me outside the restaurant where her legal lunch club is meeting. When we go inside to the main banquet hall they reserved for the occasion I notice that most of the people there are female and maybe ten percent have male companions. I'm told that there are quite a few court clerks and legal secretaries in the club too. This is good. I like to know as many people in the legal community as possible, because networking is very important to professionals.

Up on the speaker's platform is a lectern with their club's seal hanging on the front - the three large letters 'L.L.B.' That's a clever monogram, because it also stands for the degree that most graduating attorneys receive... a bachelor's degree in law.

The usual rubber chicken lunch is served and plenty of gossiping goes on. One of Myra's office staff is seated at our table. She recognizes me and says hello. Maybe Patty will bring me again some time. This is nice. I get to look at a lot of females and get friendly with another prosecutor or two.

After we all finish our main course Judge Parker goes to the lectern. No introduction is necessary – everyone in the room knows who he is. He thanks the group for inviting him and does a short, half-hour speech about new case law pertaining to the use of informants. After his little talk, he tells everyone that it's time for us all to go back to work. This afternoon has been a pleasant surprise.

When we get outside and the valet brings Patty's car around to the front, I walk her to the driver's side door. As she gets in, she takes my hand. "Peter, I really enjoyed having you here with me today. Would you consider coming with me again?"

I tell her that it would be a pleasure. My big yellow Hummer is brought out just behind hers, and I see all the women standing there buzzing to each other about the new piece of meat that was brought to their luncheon today... or they were talking about the car. That's okay. It doesn't make any difference... I love being a celebrity – it's great for the ego.

Driving back to the Marina, I bask in my new celebrity status. I wish Myra had been there to see all those women ogling me.

This evening I see an old acquaintance on television. It's Special Agent Bob Snell of the FBI, holding a press conference. On the lectern in front of where he's standing, there are a group of microphones with network logos on them. Flashbulbs are brightening his face on a steady basis as he starts to make his announcement. "I'm happy to announce that we've made a major terrorist arrest late this afternoon. As the result of thorough investigation, we've uncovered what we believe is a plot to assassinate the President of the United States, when he makes his visit here to Southern California this coming July the Fourth."

85

The reporters all start to shout questions at him. He doesn't take any one of them and instead continues his prepared statement. "At this time, all I'm at liberty to say is that the person is now in custody and will be arraigned in Federal Court next week on conspiracy charges."

The phone rings. It's Myra. "Hi hon, what's up?"

"You caught a break Petey, we're not going ahead with our case against Joe Morgan."

I wish she wouldn't call me that. "That's great. Is there anything I can do to help you save face on this one?"

"No, that won't be necessary. Did you watch the news tonight? Our old friend Special Agent Snell called a press conference."

"Yeah, I saw him… and I'm glad he took my advice. He looks really nice with his hair touched up like that. What color was that suit he was wearing, Bar Mitzvah blue? By the way, how come you decided to drop the Joe Morgan case… discover that you just didn't have enough to go on?"

"Peter, didn't you hear what Snell said, or is it just me that you never listen to?"

"Yeah, I heard what he said, but I'd like to know your reasoning about the Morgan case."

"Snell's prisoner… the one who supposedly is a conspirator in a plot to kill the President…"

"Yeah, what about him?"

"Peter, that's your client Joe Morgan he's got in custody. They came and took him away from us this afternoon."

She can't be serious. Joe Morgan? Involved in a conspiracy to kill the President of the United States? Impossible.

"Myra, what are you talking about?"

"Peter, I'm only going to ask you this question once, and I'd really appreciate it if you would give me a truthful answer. Were you aware of the fact that several years ago he converted to Muslim and is now known as Yousef Mohammed?"

Oh boy. It finally hit the fan. I knew something like this would happen sooner or later. Now I can appreciate how Jack Bibberman felt when he found it out and told it to me.

I was truthful about it and told Myra that Jack had followed him to a mosque, but I didn't think that his religion had anything to do with the case. She tended to agree with me as far as her case was concerned, but in the federal case, that fact obviously plays a different part.

At the end of our conversation, she tosses another question at me. "Pete, I understand you went to a luncheon today with my old boss' niece. How come you did that?

"Simple, my dear. Unlike my previously spurned romantic efforts towards the District Attorney's office, the City Attorney's office finds me quite irresistible. And if you must know, I think she likes me. She invited me to join her at next month's meeting too. I think there's a chance for a relationship there."

"I think not."

"Ah, jealousy rears its ugly head. And why, pray tell would you not consider that she might find me attractive?"

"Peter, do you know the name of her organization?"

"Yeah, they had a big sign hanging on the front of the lectern... L.L.B."

"Do you know what it stands for?"

"Of course I do. It's the bachelor of law degree that we all got when we graduated law school."

"Guess again, dummy. On their sign it stands for Lesbians' Legal Branch."

7

Nothing ever seems to work out for me. I only had two things going for me and they both went into the dumper. Joe's case would have been a winner at trial in the State court and now it's a federal case. I haven't the slightest idea what prompted Snell to make the bust, but I've got an appointment to see him tomorrow, so I'll probably find out, unless he clams up and hides behind some 'national security' blanket.

As for my relationship with Patty Seymour, I find it hard to believe she's a lesbian. I have nothing personal against them, but it's seems like such a waste to see what could be my lust interest lost to another female. Come to think of it, there must be some special gene in that family, because when her uncle was the District Attorney, he got caught in a compromising position with a young male law clerk. It's a good thing that I'm the one that caught him, or it might have leaked out. Next time I speak to Patty, I'm going to have to ask her if she's really a lesbian or if I've got a chance with her - as soon as I figure out how to ask a question like that.

Stuart calls to let me know that Olive graduated driving school and passed her driving test. When she gets her license, I'll take it back to the West Los Angeles courthouse to start her expungement process and it'll give me a chance to see Patty Seymour again. I don't know what to say, but I'm sure something will come out of my mouth... it usually does.

He also tells me that the car shipments are still coming in regularly and everything's going along just fine... he hasn't found one body in a trunk. After Myra's office retrieved that corpse from Victor's place, their CSI lab did its examination and his car's been released to him. The bodywork has already begun on its front end.

I've been going through all those reports that Jack B. brought back from New Jersey, and they still look too good to be true. I instruct Jack to start making some phone calls back east to see what the insurance companies can tell him about that I.R.S. company - like who's involved in it, how the insurance company found them, how much they get for each car sold, and anything else he can think of that might help us.

The phone rings. It's Indovine's office calling. He lets me know that I'm still on retainer to defend Joe Morgan through the federal criminal case. I guess that the dealership feels having had a terrorist on their payroll makes for bad publicity, so they're pitching in on the defense fund. Now all I've got to do is find out why he was grabbed by Snell. I can't believe that desperation for news coverage has anything to do with his busting Joe the Muslim.

Snell welcomes me into his office, but we both know it's not a social call. He thinks he's got a real serious terrorist in custody. There is no small talk between us. He starts right in.

"Sharp, I think we can put your guy away for a while on this one. First of all, we found out that he's a Muslim named Yousef Mohammed. We don't know if he was trained by Al Queda in Afghanistan or not, but if he was, we'll find out about it soon enough.

"Second, those big Suburbans he's been specializing on at that dealership for the past several years are the exact same models used by the Treasury Department in the Presidential motor caravan. They usually carry a Secret Service detail and the group of reporters who fly with the President on Air Force One. Sometimes the President actually rides in one of the Suburbans, while a decoy rides in the Presidential limo, but that information is never released, so I'd appreciate your discretion.

"Thirdly, his experience as a Navy Seal means he can rig explosives, and the past month demonstrates that he knows his stuff.

"He probably didn't intend to kill those two women, but explosives are funny things some-times, and now that they're dead, he's stuck with that too. Our experts tell us that those explosions were just practice. He was rehearsing for the real thing."

With an imagination like that, he should be working at the studios writing screenplays. I've heard of a 'stretch' before, but this one is gigantic.

"That's a nice theory, Snell, but you and I both know that vehicles in the Presidential motorcade are all flown in by military transport planes in advance of Air Force One. They're maintained by the Secret Service and never get near the dealership where my client works. How do you think he was going to pull this assassination off?"

"You're right. They are flown in, but we can't ignore the coincidence that he makes three vehicles identical to the Secret Service cars explode. Some way, some how, we believe he and whatever group he's working with planned to either get a Trojan horse into the motorcade or sabotage one of the existing motorcade vehicles. And by the way, the dealership he works at actually is on the list of approved dealerships, should one of the Secret Service Suburbans need emergency repairs. It all ties in too close together. We can't ignore this one – there's too much involved here to be a series of coincidences – the odds are too great against it."

"I hear you Snell, but if my memory serves me correctly, during the last century, a couple pulled off a robbery. They were described as being a black male and a blond white female, and they were seen driving off in a pink Cadillac convertible.

"Later that day, a black male and a blond white female were stopped. They were driving a pink Cadillac convertible. The police searched the trunk of their car and found the stolen goods. They wound up getting convicted."

"That's a nice story Sharp, but what could it possibly have to do with this case?"

"They appealed their conviction on the grounds that there was no probable cause to arrest them. The police testified that they searched the vehicle because the odds against a couple matching that specific description and driving a pink Cadillac convertible were too great to ignore, so they stopped the vehicle and searched it. And you know what? The Appellate Court agreed with the defendants. They held that the conviction should be reversed, because the police shouldn't be working on a system of odds. They're not in the gambling business, they're supposed to enforce the law. So forget about the odds against coincidence...you've got to have some definite proof."

Our discussion ends like so many do. There was no right or wrong, because things in the law are not that black and white. He still believes he saved the President's life, and I still believe he's making a big mistake. There's no way we can settle the difference between us. That's what courts and juries are for.

Joe will be arraigned in the Federal Court and it looks like we'll have to take this one all the way to trial.

Jack couldn't find anything out about any company named I.R.S. in New Jersey. I call Stuart to ask how he pays for the cars, figuring that the best thing to do is follow the money. Stuart tells me that he's instructed to have cashier's checks made out directly to the insurance company, giving us another dead end. Could this mean that I.R.S. is a division of the insurance company? I don't think so. That would be a big conflict of interest, and the New Jersey Insurance Commission wouldn't let them get away with it.

A few more phone calls to the insurance company only gives us the name of their I.R.S. contact, who is the same guy named Billy who Jack met with when he was in New Jersey pretending to be a prospective customer.

Here in California there's a Department of Motor Vehicle regulation requiring people who sell more than a specific number of vehicles in any twelve-month period to have a dealer's license. That way their actions can be monitored and the public protected. But there are a lot of people here who get around that rule by doing what we call 'passing the pink.' The free and clear title to automobiles in California at one time was printed on pink paper, so even though the colors have changed over the years, the nickname of 'pink slip' still is used.

The way that hustlers maneuver around being required to get a license is by never registering the vehicles in their own name. They buy a car from someone, have that seller sign off on the pink slip, but leave the date blank. They then keep the signed pink slip in a safe place until they find a customer for the car. The new customer takes the pink slip to get it registered, and because the original owner signed off on it, the DMV treats it as a direct sale from the original owner to the new buyer. The middleman's name never appears anywhere – all he does is pass the pink from his seller to his buyer.

If I.R.S. is doing the same thing in New Jersey, it could be a reason why they don't appear to exist. I tell Jack to contact New Jersey's Vehicle Registration Department to find out what the rules are there.

Stuart never fails to amaze me. He owns two armored trucks and his warehouse usually has at least five or six Camrys or Accords for sale. But that apparently isn't enough rolling stock for him, so he decided to go out and buy himself a brand new Lincoln Town Car for his own personal use. That must be the one that Olive was referring to earlier.

This subject hasn't come up in our recent conversations because I think he's worried that if people knew about this new acquisition, he might be thought of as a person who is into excessive conspicuous consumption, like so many other people in Southern California. When I ask what prompted him to expand his fleet, his answer is quite reasonable. "I want a car that's comfortable to sit in. The armored trucks are out of the question, and for some reason, I don't find the Toyotas, Altimas or Hondas the right fit for me, so I shopped all over town and sat in every model until I found one that fit just right." He asked me what I would be riding in if I were a multi-millionaire.

That's an easy one to answer. "A back seat." He accepts my answer and goes on to say that the reason he's calling now to tell me about his new car is because he's having some problems with it that the dealer can't seem to fix properly. He's afraid he's stuck with a 'lemon.'

This can be a fate worse than death for someone who is really into cars. You keep bringing it back to the dealer with the same complaints, they keep telling you the problems have been taken care of, and you discover that the car is exactly the same as it was before you brought it in. Stuart's main problem is that the gas gauge doesn't accurately show how much fuel the car has. Sometimes a full tank will show as completely empty, or visa versa. This can be a real pain in the neck, and Stuart wants very much to have it fixed. After the third time at the dealer, they claim to have installed a completely new sensing device. When Stuart filled up the tank and took it for a test drive, the needle did a nosedive towards empty. Now he's beside himself with disappointment and wants me to do something for him.

They never gave us a lecture about automobile lemons at the unaccredited night law school I attended. Well, maybe they did, but I wasn't there that night. Therefore, the only answer available to brilliant legal researchers like me is the Internet... and I'm not disappointed. After less than an hour of surfing, I've become an expert in the field and tell Stuart that if he wants to buy me dinner at the Charthouse, I'll give him all the legal advice he can handle. It's a deal.

During dinner, I let him know something he may have suspected for some time – that I'm good for nothing. What I actually mean to tell him is that it probably won't cost him anything for me to represent him in this matter because the California Lemon Law includes a provision for the claimant to recover most of his legal fees. And, if we're successful, the dealer will either have to refund his purchase money or replace the car with another one.

"That's great Pete, but what happens to the car they get back from me? Does some other sucker get stuck with it when they re-sell it?"

Good question. The law also provides for returned lemons to have their titles 'branded,' so that as long as the vehicle exists, it is identified as a 're-purchased lemon.'

So far, so good. Stuart wants to get started with legal action against the dealer, but the dealer's responsibility only goes as far as trying to fix the problems. When it comes to a purchase or exchange, that liability falls on the manufacturer, if the car qualifies as a lemon under the law. I tell him that for his car to officially be classified as a lemon, a couple of conditions must be met. First of all, within eighteen months of the purchase, the same defect must have been subject to repair at least four times – all with no success. They also require the problem to be a 'material defect,' but since Stuart's problem substantially impairs the use, value or safety of his car, it qualifies there too.

While we're outside the restaurant waiting for the valet to bring Stuart's car around, I can't resist asking him. "Stuart, I received a credit reference request from a Las Vegas hotel. You're not into gambling now, are you?"

He laughs. "No Pete, but I do love those big buffet spreads they have up there, and in order to be invited to the real fancy ones, they want to believe that you're a high roller, so I filled out a credit app to let them see that I'm a man of means."

This is all interesting. Stuart purchases a Lincoln Town Car, drives it to Las Vegas for buffet lunches, Vinnie is doing some hush-hush work on the car, and Stuart thinks it's a lemon. Something is wrong with this picture, but I haven't got the time or mental energy to work on it right now.

I take Stuart's car file back to the boat with me to prepare for the claim procedure but don't plan on filing it immediately until I get some more questions answered. Aside from the fact that Stuart may be making a phony claim, this is a pleasant relief for me because on this case the only thing involved is a gas gauge. No one is in danger of going to jail or losing the family house. No one is being dragged into court for violation of an order, and there's no hardship involved. It's a piece of cake, and from what I've learned about these cases, there are more than fifty thousand of them every year... and that's not counting motorcycles, RV's, and mobile homes. Vehicle lemon claims are second in number only to home improvement complaints.

I turn this matter over to our office manager and let her know that we won't be spending a lot of time on this case because there are time limits involved I also make a suggestion that our office staff have a heart-to-heart talk with Olive about the work on Stuart's car that Vinnie's been doing. If we do file a claim for Stuart, the manufacturer has 30 days to comply with our formal legal demand. Once we've accepted a satisfactory offer, it takes approximately another 15 to 30 days to return the vehicle and receive payment from the manufacturer. She grumbles an acceptance and takes the file.

This is a strange set of circumstances. I admit to not being too good a driver, and am not particularly fond of automobiles, but just about everything I've gotten involved with for the past month or so has had something to do with vehicles. There was Olive not knowing how to drive, Shirley driving drunk, Olive crashing into a police car, three exploding Suburbans, a guy accused of making car bombs, Stuart's allegedly legit used car operation, and now the lemon law. When all this stuff is over I think I'll change my concentration over to yachts... you meet a higher class of people that way. Maybe I'll even meet my neighbor George.

8

During the past few days my email inbox has received some strange messages. Two were from local police agencies offering assistance if I need fingerprinting services – for a small fee. There was one from some casino in Las Vegas because Stuart used me as a credit reference. Another two were from organizations I never heard of with alphabets in their names, and more were congratulatory, welcoming me to the world of private schools.

Every lawyer in the State of California, and probably in the other states too, has already been fingerprinted as part of the process required to take the state Bar Examination, so I don't need that service. I do not attend any private school and don't intend to, unless they start giving courses in how to improve one's social life. I get the feeling that as usual, there's something going on that's being orchestrated by the kid – and when I find out, I'll probably be told what to do because she'll have had the entire plan all worked out. There's no sense in asking her, because I won't get an answer, so I figure the only way to find out what's going on is to talk to one of the people that the kid talks to, which includes the entire world, except for me.

I know she's tutoring Stuart in his law classes, still coaching Olive on driving, helping Jack B. develop some computer skills, and teaching English to some of the employees at the Chinese restaurant where she reigns supreme. She also spends hours each week on the telephone with Myra, talking about stuff in general. She's probably talked more to Myra in the past seven weeks than I did during the seven years of our marriage. This situation requires a personal evening phone call.

Bingo! I hit the jackpot on my first try. Not only is Myra home and willing to talk to me, she also knows most of the pertinent details, so I might not have to go any further in this investigation. The way she explains it, Suzi intends to be a lawyer, which is a nice ambition for a kid. The main difference between her and others her age with similar goals is that this kid is a genius and doesn't intend to wait another ten years. As for those strange messages I received, in order for her home schooling to continue, she must be registered in a private school. Her stepfather filed the proper Private School Affidavit each year with California's Superintendent of Public Instruction, but since he's passed away and I'm her legal guardian, the responsibility of the annual October filing is now mine. That explains the email messages. The testing sites that I take her to occasionally are demanded, because her grades on the home-administered exams were so high that the idiots in charge of education now require her to take the tests in a proctored situation where they can make sure she doesn't cheat. If they had half a brain, they'd realize that she's already smarter now than they ever were. The rest of her plan involves passing the well known GED, a

General Educational Development test that was created in 1942 during World War II to allow veterans to get a credential equivalent to a high school diploma, so that they could go on to college. It's now available to all adults – and there's the rub. In California, you have to be at least within sixty days of your eighteenth birthday in order to be eligible to take the test. The kid has figured out a way around that rule by talking to a company in the state of Maryland that specializes in preparing students to take the GED. They also administer the test, and their age requirement states that you can be under the age of eighteen, but you must have written permission from the principal of your school. It finally dawns on me that I'm being set up as the principal of her school, so she can fly to Maryland some afternoon, pay them five hundred dollars for the course that she didn't take, and sail through their exam to get a high school equivalency certificate.

This alone is a tremendous task she designed, but it doesn't stop there. I see by the packages being delivered from Amazon.com that she's now preparing for her Law School Admissions Test. The LSAT is a half-day standardized test required for admission to all of the 201 law schools that are members of the Law School Admission Council. It provides a standard measure of acquired reading and verbal reasoning skills that law schools can use as one of several factors in assessing the applicants. The test is administered four times a year at hundreds of locations around the world.

Evidently, her research has determined that with a high school equivalent certificate and a high enough grade on the LSAT, she can get admitted to a law school – and if whatever small private law school she picks shows any hesitation in admitting her, she feels positive that a one-hundred thousand dollar donation to the school will sway their decision-making process. If she really wants to impress someone, all she has to do is show them how she spends her spare time working crossword puzzles in those Chinese newspapers she picks up at the restaurant. I like to work the ones in the TV Guide, so I know how hard they can be, but completing one in Chinese is something else. She always has some Asian newspaper under her arm when we go somewhere in the car, so she can catch up on current events during the trip. I guess she thinks it's better than having a conversation with me.

The State of California has some minimum age requirement for qualification to take the Bar Exam, but I'm sure the kid has some way figured out to pass another state's exam and then get licensed here on the reciprocal rules our Bar has. If she pulls all of this off, I think I'll be out of work in the next couple of years. I don't care how smart she is, there's a heck of a lot to learn in law school to pass the Bar exam, and she'll have to spend the full three years doing it. That means I've got until she's about fourteen years old before I get the axe from this law firm, but in the meantime I still have to drive her around if she wants to go more than the few blocks she dares to drive in her electric cart. And that's exactly what I'm expected to do tomorrow afternoon, because she's got another appointment toward the goal of her master plan.

I see the dog getting ready for a ride. The kid is instructing him to behave in the car, so I guess he's joining us today. Our trip will include dropping the Saint Bernard off at a grooming parlor for his bath and trim, while we go to her appointment. I'm told that I'll have to wait about an hour for her while she breezes through some silly test they want her to take. I have a hunch that the test she's taking today is one that they administer to children in grades five through twelve. According to some literature I saw lying around the boat, they allow five hours for this test, so that's why she probably thinks it'll take her almost a half hour. I bring some transcribed reports along to read while waiting. Sure enough, she returns to the car in less than forty-five minutes, leaving behind what I'm sure is a room full of stunned educators.

On the way back to the grooming parlor my cell phone rings. It's Eaton, the dealership's general manager. He claims that it's important and wants me to stop by the dealership. The cell phone is mounted on my dashboard and its speakerphone is on, so the kid hears the manager's request and shrugs her shoulders – probably a signal to let me know that the dog won't be ready for a while, so it's okay to go to the dealership. As we pull up to where I'm supposed to meet Eaton, Suzi reaches into the glove box, removes the recorder, puts on a pair of headphones and hops into the back seat. It looks like while I'm talking to Eaton she plans on making notes for the next billing statement.

Eaton gets into the car and looks toward the back seat. "Who's that?"

"She doesn't bite… don't worry about her."

"Well, I'd like to talk to you about the legal case against the dealership, and we might get into some private information." He notices she's sitting there with a set of earphones on, while reading a Chinese newspaper. "Does she speak English?" I don't want to lie to him, but I also don't want to ask her to get out of the Hummer – mainly because she probably wouldn't. Instead, I try to get around the situation. "She lives on my dock and I was just taking her to an appointment. I haven't heard her say anything in English to me today, so I guess that if you want to talk to her, you'll have to learn Mandarin."

It probably is okay for her to be present if Eaton wants to talk about the dealership's case, because technically, Suzi is part of my legal staff. I glance in the rear view mirror and notice that she's flipping a switch on the recorder. Eaton is obviously satisfied that the kid is no risk to him. Anyone who doesn't know better would think that even if she did speak English, any kid wearing earphones is probably more interested in whatever passes for music nowadays that's going through the wire to her ears than anything that a couple of old guys might be talking about. "Sharp, I want you to tell me exactly where the insurance company is in its investigation of those Suburban explosions... especially the one that killed my dear wife and mother-in-law."

This takes me by surprise. I don't blame him for being concerned about his loss, but it's a little out of the ordinary for him to be confronting me like this. "Mister Eaton I turn my investigative reports over to my client. If you're interested, you should contact the insurance defense firm or the detectives investigating the accident. Maybe they'll help you out."

This isn't good enough for him. He's agitated at my reluctance to talk to him. "Listen Sharp, I'm part of this dealership, and you represent us in this whole explosion mess. And what's more, the insurance company is paying you to represent Morgan, the defendant. I think you know more about the case than those others do."

"Well Mister Eaton, to be quite honest, I don't think that Joe Morgan is guilty of anything. In fact, the finger of guilt actually points more to you than to him."

This makes him start to go ballistic. I was afraid that the kid would get scared when he started to shout at me, but a glance in my mirror shows her to be working a crossword puzzle and ignoring us completely. Damn! I hope I never have to play poker with her.

I think that Eaton doth protest too much at my accusation. I go on to explain that Joe Morgan really had no motive to kill anyone. He may not have been happy with the fact that his warranty scam was over, but that's not a motive for murder. On the other hand, collecting on a million dollar life insurance policy is... and I tell Eaton that the insurance company informed me that he already put a claim in to collect for his wife's death.

There are certain times when you just can't think as clearly as you'd like, and being cold, tired, jealous, hungry, under stress, in pain, or angry can definitely cause a mistake in judgment. In Eaton's case, it's rage.

"Only a guy like Morgan could make that right front caliper go after that exact number of miles, and you'll never be able to prove anything against me. And I know the conspiracy laws, so even if you think I'm involved with Morgan, without his testimony against me, there can't be a conviction. Not just on a co-conspirator's uncorroborated testimony."

I'm impressed that he claims to know so much about a law that means very little to most of the public. Before he storms out of the car, he lets out one last tirade. "Besides, you represent me and this dealership, so anything I've said to you here today is a privileged communication." Then, his rage seems to cool down and with a grim smirk on his face he finishes up the conversation. "Six months from now, I'll be on some beach in the south of France, so you can take your theories and you know what you can do with them. You'll never be able to prove anything against me, and if you ever figure out what happened to my wife, I'm sure you'll appreciate true brilliance."

With that last statement, he exits the Hummer. I look in my mirror at the kid and she winks at me. I don't know what language that wink is in, but it tells me that she got the whole conversation on tape. I'm not sure about the legality of what she did, but we're the only two people in the world who know that the tape exists, and I'm pretty sure that the kid will never tell anyone.

We pick up a much smaller and nicer smelling dog and head back to the boat. He hops into the front passenger seat and is riding with his head up and out of the open sunroof. Suzi made sure that I put the dog's 'Doggles' on him first. Those are special dog goggles designed to protect his eyes from flying road debris. We get plenty attention as we drive down the street like this, because he looks like some World War I air ace, with his aviator-style goggles on and those big ears flopping in the wind.

The kid is still in the back seat working on her Chinese crossword puzzle and I'm still trying to process what Eaton was talking about. He mentioned the word 'caliper,' but I don't have the slightest idea of what that means. I speak a memo out loud, supposedly directed to the recording device, but really meant for the kid to hear. "Memo to office – try to get police report details on what could have possibly caused his wife's car to go off the road – other than the explosion."

After dropping off the dynamic duo at the boat, there's still time for me to beat the rush hour traffic and get downtown to visit with Joe Morgan. When he's brought into the interview room, his spirits are high. He's been following his case in the newspapers and realizes that the government really doesn't have much against him. To his surprise, I seem more interested in the one question I ask him than I am in his case. "Joe, what the hell is a caliper, and does a Suburban have one?"

He's surprised to hear that word 'caliper' exists in a lawyer's vocabulary. Without asking why I want to know, he goes on to explain that yes, the Suburban does have calipers. They're part of the car's braking system, and they work like C-clamps to pinch the pads onto the rotor. Brake hoses connect the caliper to the brake lines that lead to the master cylinder.

"Joe, if something happens to the right front caliper of a Suburban, what happens to the vehicle?'

"Nothing, until you step on the brakes. With only the left front caliper functioning, the left front wheel will brake to a stop while the right front wheel keeps going. The result is a sudden drastic left turn. A high vehicle like a Suburban, going fast enough, will flip over and roll... and that's not good."

I tell Joe not to worry about his case, and I make a hasty exit. All the way back to the Marina I keep thinking about what Eaton said. He obviously knew that his wife's right front caliper wasn't functioning – now all I have to do is find out who else knows that fact about the accident, because if nobody else knows but Eaton, then I think we've got a murderer on our hands – but with absolutely no way to prove it. The thing that really worries me is Eaton's implying that Morgan will keep his mouth shut. Could that mean that Joe did the dirty work and is keeping quiet because he thinks he can beat the case and get a big payoff from Eaton when the insurance and probate money come in?

I've been dealing with criminals for over twenty years now, and I think I can tell when a client is lying to me. Unless he's really a good actor, I don't think Joe's lying. I think he's really innocent of this whole thing. Jack Bibberman is going to have some work to do, because I want to know everything about Eaton's whereabouts during the time those three Suburbans were being serviced at the dealership.

Returning to the boat, I see that the NJPD has returned a package to me. It's the stuff we sent them on that corpse in the trunk - the bullet, picture, dental records, and fingerprints. Also included is a note thanking us for our efforts and saying that he's not anywhere in their system. Another dead end. Myra always thought that it was a back East case, so she never got her department too involved in it. I don't want to bother her, so I send a message to the kid, telling her to use some connections with the local uniforms that eat at the restaurant every day. Maybe they can find out something about this stiff. Sometimes one police agency can have info that the others don't have. One of these days they should figure out some way for them to talk to each other by computer. Maybe then the closed-to-unsolved file ratio will increase.

A sure sign of success in many circles is having your last name spoken as only a vowel. To qualify for this distinction one must meet several criteria. First, your last name must be a minimum of four syllables and be too troublesome to be pronounced in any normal conversation. Second, the name must end in a vowel. Third, you must have a large stomach and accentuate it by wearing golf shirts - and you get extra points for being of Mediterranean ancestry. The owner of I.R.S. meets all of the requirements. He is referred to as Billy 'Z,' has quite a colorful background and probably looks very much like Tony Soprano. Our own Jack B.'s title is exempt, because I'm the only one using it.

In the years of his life that would normally be dedicated to high school, Billy was a door-to-door canvasser for an aluminum siding company. In just a few years, he became the owner of his own home improvement firm and was indicted for defrauding homeowners. They alleged that his salesmen were instructed to use what was called 'the model home pitch,' whereby a customer was led to believe that the work on their home would be free. They were told that signing the sales contract was merely a formality, because payments for their five thousand dollar home improvement job would be made from commissions on other sales in the neighborhood. At one time, he had over twenty 'tin men' selling jobs throughout New Jersey. For some strange reason, none of the defrauded victims would testify against him, so there was no conviction.

After his acquittal, Billy entered the business of high finance - he opened up a loan company that charged exorbitant interest and could have been affiliated with showbiz, because of their 'break a leg' motto some of his collectors were known for. He specialized in loans to owners of construction companies who had difficulty paying their gambling debts. As a result of a brilliant system of bartering, Billy Z was able to build a large warehouse for less than one-tenth of the normal construction cost. When his debtors couldn't pay their weekly installments, Billy would take it out in lumber and other building supplies.

With a large empty warehouse, Billy's next idea was to fill it with stolen automobiles that had been recovered. Billy collected a reward from the insurance company for returning each vehicle to them prior to the time when the policyholders were due to be paid for their loss. Unfortunately, some of his street personnel suffered from 'pre-mature recovery,' and were arrested for picking up vehicles before they were reported stolen – a troublesome technicality. When the insurance companies decided to stop paying rewards to him for return of stolen cars, coincidentally there was a drop in the auto theft rate in New Jersey. Billy kept adding to his inventory and decided to start selling them on the open market. In addition to recoveries, he was buying 'lemons' that had been re-purchased by the factory from unsatisfied customers.

When Jack B. called several of the insurance companies that Billy Z has business relationships with, he learned that the companies dealt with two different I.R.S. firms. In one of them, the letters stood for Insurance Recovered Vehicles. The other use of the acronym was for Interstate Repossession and Salvage, a firm that dealt in completely wrecked cars to be crushed for salvage purposes.

While sorting through the maze of companies that Billy Z operates, the details of an elaborate scheme started to surface. The records showed that I.R.S. only dealt with Toyota Camry's and Honda Accords. These are probably the two most popular cars sold in the United States and they therefore have the highest theft and accident rates. By hacking into New Jersey's Vehicle Records, one of our office staff was able to determine a curious coincidence in the I.R.S. purchasing quantities. They buy the exact same number of wrecks as the total number of returned lemons and stolen cars recovered. Also interesting is the fact that they register the lemons purchased first, and then the wrecks to be crushed.

Taking all of this data, along with the coincidence into consideration, I give Jack B. the most important assignment of all. He's to call the owners of every wrecked, recovered stolen, and lemon that I.R.S. purchased during the past two months, and ask only one question: "what color was your car?" When all the answers are collected, he's to make a chart that compares them to a chart of the I.R.S. registrations with the New Jersey Motor Vehicle Department.

Jack starts on his new task immediately. The thing he really likes about it is that he can do it from the comfort of his living room. Not being the type of person who likes to get up early in the morning, on this assignment he can make most of the calls after four in the afternoon. The calls are all being made to the East Coast, so between four and five here is dinnertime there, with a higher success rate of getting the requested information. I have a hunch I know what Billy Z is up to, but can't be sure without Jack's completed charts. Finally the information is complete, and we discover a series of amazing things taking place that would rival the tricks of a world-class magician: the cars are changing colors – and not one ounce of paint is being used. The color change is done in Billy Z's computer.

If you look at a vehicle description on any state's ownership paperwork, you will see that it contains the Vehicle Identification Number, or 'VIN.' It also will have the year of manufacture, model, and assigned license plate number. It will not have the vehicle's color, and this lack of statistical information is what gave Billy Z what he must have thought was his most brilliant idea of all. He would switch the VIN from one vehicle with another to enhance its sale value.

Like California, quite a few states have enacted legislation that requires manufacturers who re-purchase 'lemons' from customers to label or 'brand' the title with the information that the vehicle was turned back due to a failure to perform required repairs. This label stays with a vehicle's title, no matter what State it's subsequently registered in, and greatly reduces the wholesale value – sometimes as much as fifty percent, notwithstanding the fact that the factory offers an additional warranty.

After putting together the pieces of Billy Z's jigsaw puzzle, it looks like he's buying a total wreck that matches the titled description of each lemon and recovered stolen that he purchased. He then switches Vehicle Identification Numbers, using the wrecked VINs on the lemons, and visa versa.

The salvage yard doesn't care if the car being crushed was a lemon or not – all they're interested in is the weight. By buying a total wreck and then selling it for junk, Billy has the opportunity to increase the value of each lemon by as much as five to eight thousand dollars, and make it look like the lemon was crushed and the total wreck was miraculously restored to a sellable condition.

Toyota and Honda cars rate quite high with customers, so the lemon rate is quite low. Billy makes up for this by putting VINs from the wrecks onto the stolen cars that he buys at police auctions, thereby raising their values considerably also.

Billy didn't want any trouble in his back yard, so the re-numbered lemons were sold out of state, to dealers like Stuart, who thought that their deals were too good to be true. This is a great ironic twist. Stuart was upset because he thought his Town Car was a lemon. He never realized that most of the cars he was buying and selling were probably lemons.

Jack B. works for Stuart and I don't want him to keep this secret from his friend and employer, so to avoid any awkward situation, I'm purposely keeping Jack out of the loop on this final analysis of Billy Z's business practices. I'll take care of Mister Z in my own inimitable style. In the meantime, Stuart should be told that he may have some lemons mixed in with the recovered stolen cars. I arrange to meet with him, and this time dinner is on me at the Charthouse. It's a beautiful warm summer evening and they've got some new dining furniture on the patio, which is less than ten feet from the seawall and the boats... and from there I can see my beautiful Grand Banks. If I see George walking by, I'll invite him to join us for dinner.

Stuart gives his Lincoln Town Car to the car-parking valet and we decide to have a drink at the bar while waiting for our outside table to be cleaned off and prepared. Once inside the restaurant I tell my usual waiter Brian that he should prepare my special chopped salad, which consists of the standard lettuce and tomato with some extra garbanzo beans, white onion, garlic, anchovies, and mushrooms. He does a great job of making it. Instead of the usual salad dressing, he brings a small cup of crushed garlic and olive oil. I'm sure the extra few dollars in his tip is a major inducement for this kind personal service I get here.

118

Once Stuart and I are both seated at the bar I try to start as casually as possible, because the things he's going to hear might upset him. "Stu, I want to talk to you about lemons."

"Thanks, Pete, but we've already had this discussion, and I don't see any reason to re-hash things. It's true that Vinnie did a little work on the Town Car. If his screwing around under the dashboard caused my gas gauge to malfunction, I can live with it." I knew it. I always thought there must have been some way that Vinnie was involved. I'll bet that Stuart was probably trying to have the car's odometer disconnected, so his frequent trips to Las Vegas wouldn't put him over the car's factory warranty limit.

"That's a healthy attitude Stu, but I'm not talking about the Lincoln... I'm talking about all those cars you've been buying from back East and having trucked out here." This takes him by surprise. I wait until he's had time to finish his first drink, because he'll take my news a little easier with some booze in his system.

I give him a full report. Everything that Jack found out, all about Billy Z's background, conversations with the owners about color, the fact that half the owners talked to didn't have their car stolen – they were either bought-back lemons or total wrecks. Stuart doesn't say a word. He just sits there quietly, sipping on his drink and taking it all in. When I finish my report, he remains silent for a while, and then finally gives me his opinion.

"Good. Really good. I've got to hand it to him. The plan is a stroke of genius. I'm sorry that I was on the short end of the stick, but I have faith in you to straighten everything out. I just think that the son-of-a-gun deserves some credit for thinking that plan up."

I'm amazed that he's taking this so calmly. I guess that Stuart's devious mind realizes that it takes talent to recognize genius, and Stuart recognizes it in Billy Z's plan. "Okay, Pete, what do we do to him? I want to stay in business and keep buying cars at a decent price, so let's not queer the deal... but we've got to let him know that we're on to his scam and he's got to make it right for me."

"I'm working on a plan Stu, but first of all you have to be protected from actions by your own unhappy customers. Now that we have the real VINs on the cars you bought, we can get the answers as to what each car's problem was and why the manufacturer's bought it back. Once that's done, we can enter that info on each of your customer's files. If any one of them contacts you with a problem like that, we won't be able to get any satisfaction out of the manufacturer, because Billy Z altered the VIN. That means he'll have to take care of the problem himself. This scenario is unlikely, because I've been told that when the factory re-purchases a car they fix the problem in a way that the dealer was unable to, so the lemons you sold were actually in pretty good condition."

"What about the recovered stolens?"

120

"That's another story. Their warranties were also voided by Billy Z's alterations, but being such well-manufactured cars to begin with, you shouldn't have any problems. Just in case though, I'd make some connection with a Japanese car repair place, just to keep your customers happy if some problems crop up. I'm sure we can convince Billy Z to make some reparations."

A dangerous sign appears, indicated by the expression on Stuart's face. It's like a light bulb going off over his head.

"Peter, I've got it. We'll file a class action against Billy Z."

"Nice idea Stu. That'll give him some incentive to keep selling cars to you."

"Can't we make it part of the settlement that he has to keep providing me with product?"

"Sure, after we clean out every penny he has to his name, I'm sure he'll want to keep buying cars to ship out here for you."

"Okay, we won't put that requirement in there... do you think we've got a case?"

"Sure you've got a case... if you've bought thirty-five cars from him with altered VINs, he's defrauded you a bunch of times, but you've made money on each of the sales. How big are your damages?"

"Aren't I entitled to something just for being defrauded?"

"Yeah, but it probably wouldn't be enough to cover the losses you'd incur by being put out of the used car business."

"Then what about a class action on behalf of every person he sold an altered car to?"

I hate to admit it, but he might have a point there. The only problem is collectibility. If Billy Z is as sharp as Stuart gives him credit for, he's probably got everything in someone else's name. Even if we got a judgment against him, it would be next to impossible to collect on it.

"Stu, you're probably right. There may be a good class action against Billy, but there are five things to consider in every suit like this, and I think we fall short on the last two."

"Okay professor, lay it out for me. I'm gonna be a lawyer in three more years, so it's time I learned about it."

"I'm no expert in class actions, but I believe the main things that the court looks for before certifying a class are Numerosity, Commonality, Typicality, Adequacy of Representation and Viability of the Defendant."

"I think I understand the first two. You have to have a bunch of people and they have to share some legal claim against the defendant. What's that third one Typicality about?"

"It means that if you're the lead plaintiff, you're required to have suffered the same type of damages that the others in the group did."

Stuart finally catches on. Legally, he's on pretty solid ground to be a lead plaintiff in a class action, but collecting from Billy Z is the problem.

"Pete, I agree with you. But your feeling about not being good enough in this type of lawsuit isn't justified. I think you're a good attorney."

"Thanks Stu, but don't confuse Adequacy with Competency. That portion of the require-mint just requires the lead attorney to fairly represent all the members of the class without any partiality to the lead plaintiff."

Once the law lecture ends, the rest of the evening goes quite well. Brian did a fine job of preparing my special salad, Stuart didn't go ballistic finding out he was defrauded, and he learned a little about class actions. We decide to take things as they come, treating each problem on an individual case basis. Stuart hasn't received one complaint from a customer yet, so things are looking rosy. My job now is to figure out a way to let Billy Z know that the scam is over, while still allowing Stuart to keep doing business. I'll have to think this one over for a while.

I've still got some time before Joe Morgan's case comes up in Federal Court, so as far as Billy Z. is concerned, maybe the time for thinking is over and it's now time for action, so if I don't get this mess out of the way now, I may not have time to do it for a while. I call Stuart and tell him to have his travel agent get me a first-class round trip ticket to New Jersey and back – and not to worry about the cost because Billy Z will be picking up the tab on this one. I really don't know what to say to the guy, but it's at least a six-hour flight from the left coast to the right coast, so there's still some hope. Knowing Billy's background, it will have to be handled delicately, because I don't want to get a guy like him mad at me. He's probably accustomed to having things done his way, so whatever I come up with will have to make sense to him. I value my kneecaps too much to try and force him into a deal he won't be happy with.

In my opinion, all flying should be avoided. I feel the same way about elective surgery. The only exception is when I absolutely must go somewhere beyond my five hundred mile driving limit, conveniently established to include Hummer trips to San Diego, Las Vegas, and San Francisco. New Jersey definitely requires a flight, but going first class should take some of the edge off.

The flight is pleasant, but the flight attendants aren't as attractive as they used to be when they were called stewardesses. I see that several celebrities are also on this flight in the first class area, but we seem to have made a silent agreement that if they don't bother me, I won't bother them. I remember that day at Patty Seymour's lunch seminar and can appreciate what it feels like to be a celebrity. I feel their pain.

I land in Newark and go to the car rental place to pick something up. They don't have a Hummer, so I take a Chrysler PT Cruiser. It's become the car of choice for gangs in Los Angeles, and I wanted to fit in with Billy Z's group of associates.

After less than an hour of driving, I see Mister Z's warehouse. It's amazing what one can do with the proper construction discounts. Jack B. called in advance making an appointment for me, so I'm expected. I specifically told Jack to not mislead Billy into thinking I'm there as a car buyer. I want him to believe that whatever I say is the truth, and it's a bad idea to start our meeting with a lie.

Off to the side of the warehouse is a long, low building with several open bays, like the service areas of a car dealership. Each bay contains a car in some stage of being detailed for sale. Some are up on lifts having tires, brakes, and other bottom parts worked on. At the far end of the compound is a spray booth, and there are several chain hoists for lifting engines. All the bays are full of cars and there must be at least ten people working in the seven service areas. This is some operation he's built. I'll bet it would turn a profit even if it were run as a legitimate business.

I park in an open space near the warehouse's office door and take a moment to look through the file that we prepared. It contains all of Jack's charts, lists of previous owners, flow charts showing VIN numbers and automobile colors going from vehicle to vehicle, and the final classification and disposition of each vehicle we were able to find out about, including the thirty-five that were sold and delivered to Stuart.

Inside the warehouse, the front portion is partitioned off into two or three small offices. Entering the front door one encounters a tiny reception area, with a receptionist like I've never seen before. It's a he, and he's completely ignoring me while reading what looks like some publication that lists horses in a racetrack. Without looking up toward me, he speaks. "Whatta ya want?" I was considering bringing Vinnie with me to translate. His New Joisy dialect would have come in handy. Even without Vinnie, I understand what this four hundred pound giant receptionist is saying.

"I have an appointment with your boss."

"What about?"

"It's rather personal. I'd rather discuss it with him."

One of the office doors opens and Billy Z sticks his head out. I recognize him from the mug shots. He looks much better without that number under his chin.

"You Sharp?"

When I tell him that we have an appointment, he looks at the receptionist. "He clean, Nunzio?"

Due to the time of the year and the humidity, I'm not wearing a suit or sport coat. I decided to wear a Soprano-style golf shirt and a pair of Dockers trousers. It's obvious that I'm not wearing a gun or a wire, so in Nunzio's eyes I pass the 'cleanliness' test and he grunts a yes toward Billy, who then motions for me to follow him into the office. This is good, because it's the only part of the entire building that has an air conditioner sticking out of a window. I follow his instructions and sit down opposite his desk. His opening remark gives me an idea of his sophistication.

"That little bald Jewboy called and told me you'd be comin' to talk to me. What's it about?"

So much for small talk. His description of Jack confirms my thoughts about his sensitivity and I can tell that this isn't going to be easy. I probably won't even get a chance to tell him that I met one of my father's friends back in Chicago years ago, and he was a nice guy, even though he was a gangster. Too bad, because I'm sure he would have enjoyed that story.

"Mister Z, can I call you Billy?" I take his glaring silent stare as consent to the familiarity. "Billy, I'm a lawyer from Los Angeles, and I'd like to give you about fifteen minutes of legal advice. Do you have a single dollar bill?"

He looks at me like I'm crazy, which is very perceptive on his part. Slowly, he opens his desk drawer, reaches in and removes a one-dollar chip from Donald Trump's Atlantic City Taj Mahal Casino that is lying with many others, right next to a shiny revolver. He tosses the chip onto the desk in front of me.

I pick up the chip, put it in my pocket, and start my pitch. "Billy, I hope I can trust you, because I've just broken the law."

If I had any connections with Pay-per-view, I'd arrange for a poker game between Suzi and this guy. It would be a world-class stare-off. No expressions, just straight poker faces.

"You got twelve minutes left, lawyer."

At least I know he was listening. I wonder what happens when my fifteen minutes are up. I realize I'm not in the Marina surrounded by gentlemen members of the yachting community. This place must have been the inspiration for the Bada Bing Club, and they have their own way of showing people the door.

"Billy, I'm not licensed to practice law in New Jersey, so any advice I give you can get me into trouble, because outside of California, I'm considered to be practicing law without a license. That's only a misdemeanor, but it can still get me suspended from practicing in California, and that would cost me a lot of money. Anyway, whether I'm licensed to practice here or not is beside the point. The attorney-client privilege attaches to anything said in this room, so now that you've paid me a retainer, I'm going to show you a file we've prepared."

I open the file and spread the contents down on his desk in front of him. He doesn't look down at the stuff – he keeps his eyes on me. I sit down again and go on.

"The material in that file shows exactly what you've been up to. Every recovered stolen you purchased at auction, every total wreck you bought at the salvage yard, every re-purchased lemon you took bought the factory rep, every color, every VIN, and statements from all the previous owners.

"I want you to know that the attorney-client privilege we're working under here applies to every car in this file, but it does not apply to similar acts you might commit in the future – and I'm advising you here and now to stop committing them... at least with respect to one particular customer you have in Southern California.

"Oh yeah? And who might that be?"

"Stuart Schwarzman. He's my friend and client. You sold him thirty-five cars, and we found a dead body in one of the trunks. He appreciates that free option, but would rather you didn't do it anymore."

I must have hit a sore spot by mentioning the dead body because suddenly Billy jumps up and slams his fist down on the desk in protest. The door springs open and Nunzio's head pops in. "You okay, boss?"

Billy signals that everything is under control, so the conversation continues.

"I don't think you had anything to do with that body, because we sent the bullet, dental records, and other identification to your local police agencies, and they said it wasn't a New York or New Jersey crime, so we don't have to talk about it any more."

This seems to take the pressure off a little. I now realize that I shouldn't have mentioned anything about the body. As I heard those words, I was saying to myself "what idiot just said that?" I figure there's less than nine minutes left, so I go on.

129

"As I was saying, I don't care what you do here with your cars, wrecks, and customers. All I care about is my client in Van Nuys. He's doing quite well selling those cars you send him, and he'd like very much to continue doing business with you, so here's what I'd like to suggest. First, please don't sell him any cars that have had the VINs switched. He doesn't mind buying recovered stolens or re-purchased lemons, as long as he knows what he's getting. If it's a recovered stolen, please let him know how many miles were on it when it was recovered. If it's a re-purchased lemon, please let him know what the reason for the buy-back was so he can check to make sure the proper repairs have been made. If you'll play it straight with him, he can transfer the remaining warranties over to his buyers, and everyone will be happy."

Billy continues his stare. "And what if your client isn't happy?" I now realize that the rubber has just hit the road. This is the showdown, where all the cards are laid out on the table. I take my time and make sure that this comes out right, because I don't want it to be my last words on this earth.

"Billy, we're talking about used cars here. I know that they're late models, but they're still used cars and sooner or later, one of Stuart's customers is going to experience some car problems. If we can't straighten out the problem, then the customer will sue Stuart and if his lawyer has half a brain, he'll name you as a defendant. Lawyers on breach of contract cases don't work on a contingency, they bill by the hour. That means that some schmuck attorney will be subpoenaing all the information we have that's in the file on your desk. Once the word gets out, the rest of the customers will smell blood and their attorneys will join in to make it a feeding frenzy. The only way to avoid that is to know that you'll be a gentleman and do the right thing."

"What's the right thing, lawyer. You asking for money now?"

"No Billy, I'm not asking for any money. What I'd like to know is if you'll cover Stuart's back and take back a car once in a while if the situation warrants it. You send out the replacement with an unaltered VIN, and we'll put the exchange on the truck to be brought back to you.

"That's it?"

"Yeah Billy that's it. And if you really want to be a prince, here's a copy of the invoice for my plane ticket and car rental. It would be nice if you could discount the next car Stuart buys by that amount."

The air conditioning isn't working as well as I would have liked it to, because I feel soaked in perspiration. As I slowly leave Billy's private office, I close the door behind me and politely nod towards Nunzio. This scene of me leaving reminds me of a scene in an old movie where some world war II prisoners disguised themselves as German officers and then casually strolled toward the prison's main exit. Everyone watching that film was sitting on the edge of their seats. We saw close-ups of the prison guards looking down at the phony officers, and we were afraid that the prisoners would be recognized and never make it to the gate and to freedom. Slowly walking out of Billy Z's place, I now know how those prisoners felt.

Stuart doesn't believe I pulled it off. He made me recount the whole conversation word for word, and when I tell it again for Jack and Vinnie, Stuart listens in as if it were the first time. I leave out the parts about me breaking the law in New Jersey, my intense perspiration, and also where Billy Z told me he liked the way I handled myself and would refer some business to me out here.

With the Billy Z and Stuart situation under control, I've got to concentrate on getting Joe Morgan off of the hook. I feel in my heart that he's innocent, but with the political climate being what it is nowadays, I can imagine how an experienced Federal prosecutor can turn a jury into a lynch mob - especially faced with a Muslim who is allegedly part of conspiracy to kill our President. With a convincing argument, even a jury member not in the President's political party might vote for conviction.

Somewhere in the back of my mind is the feeling that some answers are at the dealership where Joe works. My feelings about Eaton's guilt are as strong as my feelings about Joe's innocence. I certainly hope Jack B. comes up with some holes in Eaton's timeline alibi.

Gene Grossman

I drive over to the dealership to snoop around. Maybe I'll get lucky with some talkative low-level employee who has no love for his general manager.

If you've seen one new car dealership, you've seen them all. They've all got their fanciest models in the showroom, a front line of beautiful used cars that they want you to believe were traded in, and the cash cow service department with numerous repair bays and a cashier behind thick glass who's more secure than a bank teller.

This particular dealership has one extra feature that I've never noticed in any other one before – a security guard posted near a closed garage door. He isn't just one of the dealership employees wearing a jacket with the word 'security' on its back, he's a true rent-a-cop and he's wearing a gun.

I know that Vinnie and Olive carry unloaded weapons in their holsters, but they do it for show only. This guy looks like he means business. I ask a couple of mechanics if they know anything about the security guy or what he's guarding, but the only information I can gather is that the garage is 'off limits' to all customers and employees, and that I should avoid going over there. They tell me that whatever's in there was wrapped up and offloaded from a large truck, and that it was done inside the building, after the guard was posted.

Columbo is my favorite television detective. He has a method to get information out of guilty people. He just keeps dogging them until they make the mistake that shows him how to solve the case. I might as well take a page out of his book and start working on Eaton. One method Columbo uses is to ask for the suspect's help in solving the crime, so I think I'll ask if Eaton can get me inside that area that security guy is guarding. It may not help the case, but even if it's not connected in any way, my curiosity will be satisfied and Eaton will think my investigation is going in some direction other than his.

They page Eaton is over the dealership's PA system and he meets me at the service department's sign-in area. I can tell he's on his guard when talking to me. He wants to appear to be helpful, but he's got something to hide and we both know it.

I tell him that I'm curious about that security guard and would like to get into the garage to see what's so important. Eaton lets me know that there's no way I'm getting in that garage. The dealership has some contract with the Federal government for emergency repairs on their vehicles and that garage is a secure area. His answers don't sound right to me, so it's time for a little out-of-court cross-examination.

"If it's that secure, how do your mechanics get in there to work on the vehicles?"

"They don't. When a government vehicle is in there the government mechanics come to work on it. All we do is provide a secure garage facility for them."

"That's ridiculous. They've got plenty of garages in the Federal Buildings."

"Yes, they do, but the July Fourth parade will be coming down this street, and there's not a federal building within fifteen miles of this dealership."

"Are you trying to tell me that there are federal vehicles in that garage?"

My last question stops him for a second. He hesitates before answering.

"I'm not supposed to tell anyone about this, but since this is a privileged communication… it is privileged isn't it?"

"Of course it is."

"Well, it's a special vehicle that's going to be in the parade. The President might even ride in it."

"Great. Can I go in and see it?"

He can't get me into the garage. He's the general manager of the entire dealership, but he still can't break the rules that his employer agreed to. He does make one concession.

"I can't get you in there, but if you're with me, you'll be allowed to go around to the back of the building. There's a locked storage shed back there with some file cabinets, and if you can get inside it and stand on something, you can peek through a hole in the wall and see inside the garage."

"And just how do you happen to know all about this elaborate peeking procedure?"

"I have the only key to that shed, and I had to go in there yesterday to get some sales brochures. While I was in there, my curiosity got the best of me."

135

"Okay Eaton, don't make me guess... what did you see?"

"C'mon...you'll have to see for yourself."

Eaton walks with me as we approach the garage. The guard obviously knows who he is. They nod at each other as we walk by. When we get around to the back, he goes to the storage shed and opens the lock. Once inside, he closes the door again and moves an empty file cabinet away from the wall. Sure enough, there's a six-inch diameter hole with a two-inch diameter pipe coming through it, leaving some peeking room. Fortunately there was a concrete block lying around, so I bring it over, stand it on its sixteen-inch side, and step up to peek into the garage.

Eaton was right. It's not a military tank, presidential limo, or secret service Suburban. It's a red, white, and blue customized Hummer with its top removed, making it look like a huge patriotic, open phaeton. Sitting on the floor next to it is a large bubble-like plastic dome, also partially open on the top. The bubble top has some straps around it that are connected to a chain hoist coming down from the building's ceiling. They're obviously going to lift it up and attach it to the Hummer, making it a secure vehicle for someone important to ride in. I don't think there are very many of these red, white and blue four-door Hummer convertibles around, so this must be the one that Olive told me about. The nagging question now is, with all the government security, how the hell did she know about it? Of all the people in the world that the Federal government might tell about that Hummer, Olive is probably right near the bottom of the list – just above Osama bin Laden.

Driving back to the Marina, my Hummer is doing about thirty miles an hour, but my head is doing at least ninety, trying to figure out how Olive knew about it. The only thing I can come up with is probably by some article in a recent issue of the National Enquirer. There's only one way to really find out, and that's by asking her.

Olive's knowing about the Hummer certainly asks a big question, but at the same time it answers one. If that Hummer is the one that's going to be in the Presidential parade, then I think I now know what's going through FBI Special Agent Snell's mind. He isn't worried about Joe Morgan sabotaging a Secret Service Suburban or planting a Trojan horse in the parade, he's trying to protect that Hummer from a guy trained in the use of explosives.

This is interesting. Myra kept Joe locked up and didn't have a motive. All she had was a case of some people paying a service manager under the table for some non-warranty repairs. Snell has Joe locked up but has absolutely no case at all. Nada. Zip. Nothing.

I don't know any explosive experts, but my friend Victor at 1800AUTOPSY certainly should. I've heard that he brings experts like that in whenever someone gets blown up, so I call him to get a referral. He turns me on to a guy he uses who formerly worked with the LAPD Bomb Squad. I make arrangements to pick him up and take him with me to see Snell at the Federal Building. I want to see the infamous explosive device that Snell thinks can blow up a Presidential parade.

Snell agrees to meet with us at his office and I tell him that I'm bringing an explosives expert along with me. When we're shown into his office, he gets up with a smile on his face and an outstretched hand. I'm really surprised to see this, and then realize that the welcome isn't for me. Snell walks right past me and shakes hands with my explosives expert.

"Hello Vaughn, it's been a long time."

What a small world. My expert used to be with the FBI and worked on quite a few cases with Snell before retiring and working part time with the LAPD. I didn't know if their being old friends was a good thing or not until we all sat down and started talking. Snell is a smart one.

"What can I do for you today counselor?"

"I know about the bubble-top Hummer, Agent Snell."

He looks down at his desk for a while, like he's been caught being a naughty boy. I have to hand it to him – he knows that the best defense is an offense.

"Counselor, any information about whether or not a vehicle like that exists is classified. If you have some knowledge you're not supposed to have, then you're in a lot of trouble."

"Relax, super spy. I represent the company that insures that dealership, and it's my responsibility to know what's being stored in every building there. I happened to notice that flag car during a routine inspection of a shed behind the building that has a hole in the wall looking right into where the Hummer is being worked on. So now that you know I'm not a foreign agent, I'd like to get back to the commercial – my client, Joe Morgan.

"I have a hunch you realize that your friend Vaughn here will be able to tell in a New York second that the explosive devices found at Morgan's house are only good for being squibs and setting off a fireworks display. So what the hell's going on? We both know you don't have a case against my client. What's this game-playing all about? Is it just because he's a Muslim? I don't think you would take a chance like that. Am I wrong?"

He starts in slowly.

"No Peter, you're not wrong. But I'm in a real difficult position here and I'm going to break some rules by telling you what it is. I know you're a good lawyer and my past dealings with you on that bank robbery gang have shown that you're a man of your word, so I'm going to have to trust you on this one.

"You're right. The explosives we found at his house really can't do any damage, but we didn't know that when his arrest warrant was issued and we had him transferred over here from Myra's jurisdiction. Look at it from our perspective. We've got a Muslim who's a former Navy Seal. He's well trained in explosives and works at a dealership that's garaging a vehicle scheduled to be in a Presidential parade.

"Our intelligence tells us that there's a very high probability that some attempt will be made to do some damage during the parade. Secret Service tried to talk the President out of appearing, but he insisted. There are just too many voters in California for him to not show up.

"Actually, we're doing both you and your client a favor by keeping him in custody until after the parade. If we release him before the parade and some crazies kill some people that day, then you know what will happen. The press will have a field day. My head will be on the chopping block for letting a suspected Muslim terrorist with explosives training out onto the street just before a Presidential parade during which a terrorist attack takes place. Whether your client is innocent or not, he'll be picked up and sent to Cuba for interrogation, and I'll probably be fired or transferred to our field office in Nome, Alaska.

"The best thing is for him to stay in our custody, so I'll make a deal with you. He stays in, you keep quiet about it, and after the parade we'll let him out, whether there's an incident or not. You've convinced me that he's not involved in anything, so he'll be free after the parade – but I can't make any guarantees about your ex-wife. When we release him, we'll have to send him back to her. It's then her decision to make as to whether he gets released on bail. If he's not involved in anything more than some under the table stuff for repairs, then he should have no trouble bailing out."

140

"I don't really have a choice, do I? The parade's only another few days away. Even if I made a big stink I couldn't get him out before then, and if I did, and if there was an incident, then it's back to square one. Okay Snell, you win. I'll see you after the parade."

Politics sucks. As part of our deal, Snell arranges for me to visit with Joe and I explain the situation to him. Strangely enough, he agrees that it would be better for him to stay in custody. He tells me that there are some pretty angry people at his mosque, and he doesn't want anything that anyone else does to make him a hunted man. As long as the FBI knows he's not one of the bad guys, he'll just sit for another couple of days and then try to get his life back on track. He only has one question. "Do you think I can get my job back?"

That's a tough one and I don't want to lie to him, so I tell him that it's unlikely, but if he's as talented a mechanic as some of his co-workers says he is, he should have no problem getting a job somewhere else. I go so far as to tell him that I might be able to help him out there. If Stuart can't use him, then maybe Billy Z could use someone who can fix cars and blow people up. He is not amused.

Vaughn the explosive expert has years of experience when it comes to cars blowing up, so I put him in touch with Myra. The first two Suburbans that exploded were repaired before anyone could take a

141

real good look at them, but the one that went off of Mulholland drive and killed Eaton's wife and mother-in-law is still at the police impound garage. The District Attorney's people have been going over it with a fine tooth comb, but haven't found anything yet. Vaughn says that he knows those guys, so I assign him the task of looking over their shoulder. I'm especially interested in the front right brake caliper, so I tell Vaughn to play it close to the chest. We want to know if the D.A.'s techies formed any conclusions before we tip our hand and give our theories away. It's still an adversarial proceeding, and I want Vaughn to make sure he knows that he's on our side now – not theirs. Just to make sure, I check with Victor at his autopsy shop and he assures me that Vaughn is a straight shooter who can be trusted.

9

Indovine's office is calling. "Hello Peter, this is Charles." This is a good sign. We're back on a first-name basis, which probably means he wants something from me.

"What can I do for you today Charles?"

"You know, in addition to insuring the dealership, Uniman also covers many of the employees... including the general manager."

"Yeah, I know. His wife was insured with Uniman. You already told me he put a claim in for his wife's death. Was it a big one?"

"Only if you think a million dollars is big." Yes, a million dollars is a big amount, but twenty years from now people will probably laugh at the fact that someone killed for such a paltry sum. Other than see people use an old dial telephone and drive old cars, the thing that really amuses me about the old black-and-white movies is the sums of money that were motives for crime. It was quite common to see a cop suspect a husband of killing his wife or partner to collect on a five thousand dollar insurance policy.

"Okay Charles, it's big. What do you want me to do, talk him out of it?"

"If there's anything you find in your investigation that connects him to that fellow charged with planting the bomb, we'd like to know about it."

"Why certainly, Charles, but if I remember correctly, you're already paying me to clear that guy.

If I do my job correctly, then he beats the murder rap and that means there's nothing that Eaton could have done with him to cause his wife's death. Uniman will have to pay the claim, unless I find some other information that will defeat it."

"Peter, are you working on another angle?"

"Angles are my life Charles. I love angles. I can look into it, but if I save Uniman the million dollars on that life insurance claim, I want my usual ten percent reward… and as usual, I'll make sure that you get all the credit for it. Do we have a deal? Because if we do, I'll expect to have you fax me a memo, just to keep everyone honest… and Charles…"

"Yes, Peter, what else?'

"The reward will not be set off by any fees paid to me along the way for my investigative work or expenses. I get paid whether I crack the case or not."

As usual, there was nothing but a grunt on the other end of the line – but also as usual, a hard copy of the grumbling acceptance just came in on the fax machine.

Jack B. reports that he's got just about every minute of the day accounted for from the time of the first Suburban explosion to the time that Eaton's wife flipped herself off of Mulholland Drive, and her old man couldn't have tampered with any of those vehicles. Jack tells me what a dedicated manager the guy is. For the past couple of months he's been working late and closing the place up.

"Jack, do you know anything about his whereabouts after the dealership closes for the day?"

"Why, do you think he's fooling around?"

"I don't know. I'm just curious about where he goes at night."

Jack is a thorough investigator. He realizes that if the dealership's locked up for the night, there's no way that Eaton can get to the vehicles waiting there for the next day's service, but he still asks around about Eaton's evening activities – and the answers aren't very promising for our case. After work each night Eaton goes straight home, where he stays all evening, unless going out to the market for some desserts for the family. I ask Jack where Eaton lives and learn that it's at least a half-hour away from the dealership.

This is not going to be easy. My main suspect was nowhere near the Suburbans that exploded. The only guy who worked on them was my client Joe Morgan, yet Eaton's wife and mother-in-law are killed in a mysterious accident. What's wrong with this picture?

I'm getting a little discouraged, but there's still a lot of information out there that I'm waiting for. Maybe something interesting will turn up. While I'm pondering all this, the phone rings. It's Myra, and she's got some results back in on the dead body found in Stuart's trunk. Running him through the Criminal Identification System, he came up with a rap sheet. He's a safe cracker. After doing several years in the penitentiary for that skill, he's been keeping his nose clean, and his parole officer was completely surprised when he learned of the guy's fate.

I was right. Something interesting did turn up. I call Jack B. and tell him to find out about our safecracking friend – who he hung out with, how he cracked safes, and anything else that we might be able to use. There's no good reason for a dead safecracker to be found in Stuart's trunk. I'm sure he didn't commit suicide there, so someone had to help him find his final resting place. I call Stuart to try and find out exactly where that car was from the moment it was delivered to him. He checks his records and tells me exactly what I don't want to hear. "Pete, that car was delivered to my garage and sat here for two days until I drove it to your boat that afternoon."

"Stu, how come you picked that particular one to drive that day?"

"Simple. I had about seven vehicles in the garage. I went to each one and turned on the ignition. The one with the most gas in the tank is the one I used... and you know how much I rely on a dependable gas gauge."

I know that Stuart didn't dump that body in his own trunk, so if what he says is correct, it means that the body was already in the trunk when the car was delivered to him. I've already met the guy he bought those cars from, and it wouldn't surprise me in the least if he were the one who killed the safecracker. After all, if I had to vote for anyone who might be acquainted with a person who breaks into other people's safes, it would have to be Billy Z.

Jack B. still hasn't come back with scheduling for the car carriers, but now there's only one of them that I'm really interested in.

The phone rings. It's a number I don't recognize on my caller ID.

"Peter Sharp here. What can I do for you?"

"Mister Sharp, I'd like to make an appointment to talk to you. I'm not looking for anything free... I'll pay you to meet with me."

"Okay, let's not get carried away. First of all, why don't you give me some idea of what you'd like to talk to me about, because if it's not in a field of law that I'm familiar with, maybe we can both save a lot of time and I can refer you to some other attorney."

"It's concerning the probate of a will."

"Yeah, that's what I was afraid of. All right, I'm going to give you the telephone number of the County of Los Angeles' Attorney Referral Service. You just tell them that it's a probate matter and give them your zip code, and they'll give you at least two or three telephone numbers of attorneys in your area who specialize in that sort of thing, so you won't have to travel too far."

"Mister Sharp, my name is James Berland. My wife was Ralph Eaton's mother-in-law and she died in a car crash, along with our daughter."

Wow! Talk about being surprised. Maybe next time I get a phone call from someone I don't know, I'll let him talk for a few minutes before trying to palm him off onto someone else. I tell Mister Berland that even though I'm no expert in the field of Wills, I'll be glad to meet with him – and there will be no charge for the consultation. He doesn't drive anymore, so I get his address and make an appointment to stop by and see him in an hour. He lives out in Hidden Hills, a gated community in the West San Fernando Valley. He'll leave my name with the entry gate's security guard.

I have to check the piece of paper at least twice to make sure I've got the correct address written down, because this place looks like Hefner's Playboy mansion. It's an all brick Tudor style of architecture that's probably at least six thousand square feet. I pull up the hill and into the huge circular driveway that can easily park six or seven cars. The inside is just as impressive with high, beamed ceilings, leaded glass windows, and beautiful hardwood peg and groove floors. If Mister Berland ever decides to move out, I'm sure he can rent the place out as a church.

I compliment him on the majestic beauty of his home, and he tells me that it's his 'Nobel prize.'

"You won a Nobel Prize? In what field was it?"

"No, no, Mister Sharp, I didn't win any prize, but we call it that because we owe it all to Alfred Bernhard Nobel, the man who the prize is named after."

149

Berland walks over to his library and motions for me to follow him. Inside the book-lined and richly oak-paneled room, he directs my attention to a large hand-written parchment document kept inside a glass case.

"This is a replica of the last will and testament of Nobel, executed in November of 1895, in which he directed that his entire estate be invested, with the interest to be distributed each year to leaders in the fields of Physics, Chemistry, Medicine, Literature and Peace, or what his will referred to as the 'fraternity between nations.'

"Nobel didn't make any provisions for the category in which my wife and I made our modest fortune, but he made his fortune by inventing some new explosives, and he patented dynamite in 1867. Our family built a large fireworks display organization using explosives, so we decided to dedicate this room to Alfred. Without his pioneering work in our field, we wouldn't be where we are today."

I hold back on mentioning that millions of people might also still be alive if Nobel hadn't done his groundbreaking work with explosives. My restraint is admirable. Usually I just blurt things out and spend hours later on asking myself why I said that. This time I keep my cool and let him continue.

"What I want to talk to you about is another will: My wife's. Eaton married our daughter Nancy, our only child. My wife's will leaves all of her estate to Nancy, as does mine, with one exception - unless Nancy pre-deceases either one of us. In that instance,

150

the remainder goes to the surviving spouse, which would be me.

"Now I don't want you to get the wrong idea. This isn't all about my wanting to get the money from my wife's will. We don't have any other children and there are no grandchildren. I have plenty of money, and if I do actually get any money as a result of her death, it's all earmarked for her favorite charities. She would have wanted it that way."

"Mister Berland, if you aren't interested in any financial gain, then why are we having this conversation?"

He hesitates for a second or two, and then with a very serious expression, continues on. "It's not who I want to get the money, it's who I don't want to get it.

"Because Eaton and Nancy didn't have any children, Nancy's will leaves everything to that rotten husband of hers. With Nancy dead too, Eaton will wind up with everything... and I have a terrible feeling about him... always did, from the first day that I met him."

"What can I do for you Mister Berland? I've already told you that I'm no expert in the area of Wills."

"I'm not looking for a Wills expert, I'm looking for a smart fellow who can figure out how to stop Eaton from getting all my wife and daughter's money."

"Let me get this straight. If your wife died first, then everything she has goes to your daughter

Nancy, which would now go to Eaton. But on the other hand, if your daughter died before your wife did, then your wife's estate goes to you, instead of to Eaton. Have I got it right?"

He tells me that I'm correct. I can't make any promises to him, so I ask him for a copy of his wife's Will and tell him I'll look into it. He lets me know that Eaton stands to get at least two million dollars from the Wills, and if I can figure out a way to stop him there will be a five percent bonus in it for me. He also offers to pay all my expenses plus an hourly rate for my work, win or lose.

This sounds interesting, but I really don't know that much about the law in this field. When I was going to law school, the Bar exam was based on fourteen subjects and you were required to answer questions on ten of them. The four that were considered optional were Wills, Trusts, Estate & Gift Tax, and Community Property.

Like many of the other students attending our unaccredited evening law school, we felt that a diploma from what we nicknamed the 'Betty Crocker College of Law' probably wouldn't get us into some large established law firm that specialized in the four optional subjects. We tried to cut down on our study load by becoming what were referred to as the 'big tenners,' a group of students going into the Bar exam knowing that we'd have to answer all the other questions, with no options.

As a result, I've never been involved in a Will contest, never prepared a Trust Agreement, make every effort to avoid Taxation issues, and wouldn't touch a domestic relations matter for any amount of money. I'm quite happy leaving all of that fascinating work to the Harvard grads. But now, I'm being dragged into a Will contest.

If my interpretation of the Wills are correct, all I have to do is show that Nancy Eaton died before her mother did. If I can do that, then the proceeds from Mrs. Berland's estate will go to her surviving husband, instead of to Eaton.

No problem. The car was destroyed, the bodies were cremated, and all I have to do is figure out which one of them died first in the same auto accident. No sense calling in Jack B. or Victor on this case – I need the Amazing Kreskin.

All I have to work with are some photos taken by the police accident investigation team. I'm sure that Victor will be happy to get an assignment from me to perform two autopsies from pictures of dead bodies. I call Jack B. and tell him to get all the pictures and reports on the accident that he can. I also put a call in to Snell's office because his crew was interested in the type of explosives used on that Suburban. From what Vaughn explained to me, there's always a 'signature' left behind by the bomb-maker. I don't know exactly what that means, but the explosives people say that a signature can lead them to the bad guy, so they must mean some style of bomb-making that's recognizable to the trained eye.

The parade is in just a few days. Jack B. has come through again with a copy of the complete police file on the accident that killed Mrs. Eaton and her mother. There were plenty of photos to see. The investigators are under the impression that as the Suburban smashed through the flimsy guardrail, both driver and passenger airbags deployed. They estimate that Nancy was tossed clear about half way down. Her mother was strapped in, so she rode all the way down in the vehicle.

It originally looked like an accident with no foul play suspected, so the overworked coroner's department didn't do any autopsies, especially in the absence of any request for one from the accident investigation detail.

Nowhere in the report is there any statement as to an opinion of which victim died first. Facts like that don't come into play in an accident investigation unless there's a suspicion that a driver was dead at the time of the accident, and they didn't think that was the case here.

This means I'm back at square one, with no way to help Berland with his wife's estate and no way in sight to pin anything on Eaton, notwithstanding his incriminating statements made to me in my car while the kid was listening in.

About the only thing I've got going for me right now is that Joe Morgan will be released after the parade, and if Myra can't make a case against him for planting the bombs, then he's only facing a larceny charge for the bribes. Unfortunately, Uniman's insurance company will still be on the hook for the exploding Suburbans, because if Joe didn't do it, any competent plaintiff's trial lawyer should be able to convince a jury that the dirty work was done at the dealership – either by Joe Morgan or by someone else with the access and know-how.

With no other ideas on hand, I guess it's time to try some long shots. Before starting his own private autopsy business, Victor was a lab tech and worked with Crime Scene Investigation units. One of his many duties required him to dust for fingerprints. After calling Stuart and learning where the damaged Camry is having its front-end damage repaired, I call Victor and ask him to please go over there and dust the rear of the car for prints. Whoever put the safecracker's body in there might have left something we can use. I also send him one of those gaudy, shiny business cards handed to me by Billy Z. There should be a good thumbprint on there that we can use. Maybe we'll get lucky and find Billy's prints on the trunk or on something of the safecracker's, like his wristwatch, belt, or anything else that Victor can lift a print off of.

The thing that really bothers me is that Eaton probably killed his wife and her mother, and he's going to get away with it. Looking at the big picture, it's an old scheme. Cover up one crime with some others. If my hunch is correct, the first two exploding Suburbans were a combination of experiments with the explosions and incidents to point the finger of guilt at Joe Morgan. If Eaton was behind everything, the main idea was to kill his wife and mother-in-law. That's not brilliant, it's been tried over and over again. The only difference in this case is that he may not get caught.

I can't go to Myra with my suspicions, because even if she agrees that it might be possible, there's nothing she can do without some evidence. She always was a stickler for detail.

Wait a minute. Something just occurred to me. I was afraid that a good plaintiff's lawyer could convince a jury that the sabotage on those Suburbans was done at the dealership by either Joe or someone else with access, so why don't I try to find out who else could have had the access.

I call Snell and make arrangements to visit with my client in the Federal hoosegow.

Joe isn't in a great mood, but he knows that he might be getting out after the parade, so his spirits aren't too low. The main thrust of my questions to him concerns who else but him could have possibly gotten to all three of those Suburbans while they were in the dealership for service. His answer isn't very encouraging. Whichever Suburban was being serviced was exclusively in his own service bay while he worked on it. No one else could have gotten to it because he rarely left the bay for more than a few minutes each day for a toilet break. He even sat there during lunchtime eating sandwiches that he brought in. If he didn't finish servicing a vehicle during the daytime, it would be locked up in his service bay overnight and he would complete the work the next morning. The dealership gave out free loan cars, so the customers never minded leaving their vehicles overnight for service.

I only have one other question for him. "Is it possible for someone to have gotten in there after hours and done something to a vehicle in your service bay?"

This one stops him for a minute. The average person probably would simply answer 'no way,' but Joe Morgan isn't the average person, he's a former Navy Seal who could probably have pulled off exactly what I was suggesting. At first he's momentarily taken aback at my question.

"Wait a minute, are you suggesting that I snuck back in there at night and rigged those trucks?"

"No, no Joe, I'm not suggesting that and neither is the prosecution. If you wanted to do something to those vehicles it would have been too easy for you to do it during the daytime. Nobody watches your work, so you could have done anything you wanted. There's no reason for you to pull a dumb stunt like coming back at night. What I want to know is if anyone else could have done it."

He thinks about it for a while. "Sure, I guess it's possible. After all, it's only a car dealership, not some secret government installation. They've got a fence around the service area, but anyone with some training could've gotten over it and into my service bay. Do you have someone in mind?"

"I don't know yet. Are there any security cameras in place there?"

"Yeah, they cover all parts of the outside fence. There are also some motion sensors, so if anyone tries to go over the fence, the floodlights will go on."

"Okay, lets say they didn't go over the fence. Any other way in?"

"Yeah, but they'd have to go through the main new car showroom, and that would require a set of keys to the whole place – and only three people have those keys - the dealership's owner, the general manager, and his assistant, and forget about them making copies for anyone else. The locks are all special and the keys can't be duplicated by anyone but the lock manufacturer, who won't do that without written authorization from the dealership owner."

Jack B. now has another assignment. I want to know where the assistant manager and dealership owner spent the few days during those three Suburban explosions, especially where they were each evening. If Joe didn't tamper with those vehicles during the day, then there's only one other possibility, and it had to be an inside job at night. From what I've heard, they sober up the owner of the dealership about once every month and bring him in to do a television commercial about the sales incentive du jour. I can't imagine any motive he could possibly have for rigging those cars or causing any injuries.

This assistant manager doesn't particularly care for Eaton and the feeling is obviously mutual, so he's a possible suspect too, but it's still not enough of a motive to kill Eaton's wife. The death of Nancy Eaton wouldn't get him a promotion or put any money in his pocket, so why do it? It couldn't have been a work for hire if there was bad blood between him and Eaton, so I might as well rule him out of the suspect pool.

By process of elimination, all roads lead to Eaton. I feel his guilt in my bones, but don't have the slightest idea how to prove it. The clock is ticking on this matter. If I don't come up with anything soon, the insurance company will have to pay Eaton a million for his wife's death, and the probate court will give him another two million for his mother-in-law's estate. With three million in his pocket, I have a strong feeling that he'll be giving up his day job.

10

Reports are being prepared now on a daily basis. Jack B. has tracked down the car-carrier's central dispatch office and is now waiting for information on if and where that truck stopped on its way to deliver those five vehicles to Stuart, one of which contained the dead body in the trunk.

Victor dusted the entire rear area of the Camry that the dead body was found in and all the prints that he lifted are sent to AFIS, the Automated Fingerprint Identification System that's mentioned so often on television CSI shows.

Mister Berland executed the proper release forms and our office has requested medical records for both his wife and daughter.

I've got complete files on the three Suburbans that exploded. The first two were towed back to the dealership, where Joe Morgan went through them thoroughly. Explosive expert Vaughn is examining the Suburban that went off of Mulholland Drive, and per my instructions will be closely scrutinizing the braking system and right front caliper.

Victor is inspecting all the crime scene photos of the crash, trying to find some way to determine which passenger died first.

While all of this is going on, Indovine's office keeps sending me memos warning me that Uniman Insurance is facing a deadline soon. If I don't come up with some justifiable reason for them to stall, they'll have to pay out on Ralph Eaton's claim for his wife's million-dollar policy.

The United States Government has no idea how busy I am, because they've obviously decided to interrupt my deep thoughts with their colorful Fourth of July Parade. The kid invited a whole gang over to watch it on our huge flat-panel plasma screen television set. Olive decided that the traffic would be too heavy, so she and Vinnie joined Stuart and Jack B., so we can all see the parade together and then have our own patriotic feast, all delivered and served by the Asian boys. To my pleasant surprise, Myra decides to grace us with her presence and Victor drove in from Pasadena too.

If you've seen one patriotic parade, you've seen them all. A cynic might describe this one as looking a lot like the annual Rose Parade, with military displays of troops in dress uniforms, the Marine Marching Band, the Blue Angels doing low-altitude fly-bys, and most interestingly the three-color red, white, and blue bubble-topped Hummer, containing the President of the United States.

When the Hummer appears, Olive grabs my sleeve and exclaims gleefully, "see? I told you so!" That reminds me to call her aside later and try to find out where or who she got her classified information from.

I have to admit that the parade is a splendid display of what our country is supposed to stand for. After dinner, we all go out onto the aft sundeck and watch the annual fireworks display that the Marina del Rey Chamber of Commerce puts on from nine to nine-fifteen every July Fourth evening. It elicits the usual 'oohs' and 'aahs' as the explosives go off up in the air.

There aren't too many places for guests to park their cars when visiting the Marina. The big public lot across the street is often almost completely filled by the valet car-parkers from the adjacent Cheesecake Factory, a local restaurant that was packed from the day it opened.

On the two big tourist days of the year, when people come to see the Christmas Boat Parade Day and July the Fourth fireworks, the local Sheriff patrols ease off on their strict enforcement rules and allow cars to be parked up and down the side streets that lead to the boat basins, where more than seven thousand vessels are berthed in the water. We've got the country's largest private yacht anchorage here.

The extra traffic load means that there is absolutely no driving out of the Marina until after ten those two evenings, so we were fortunate to have a group of people together who all knew each other for some time and enjoy brisk conversation. The kid talks to everyone but me. The dog hides during the fifteen-minute fireworks display, giving me a mean look afterward for not offering a lap he can cower upon. I try to make up for it by taking him for a brief walk, so I guess we're okay with each other now. He loves crowds, because hundreds of new people pet him as he walks by. When one person sees a stranger stroking his head, all the others nearby take it as a signal that he likes it, so he gets his quota of head-rubbing for the next few months filled.

It's now after eleven in the evening and the Asian boys have just finished cleaning up the boat interior. I can now sit down to relax and get ready for bed, and maybe some peace and quiet to plan some strategy for handling Joe Morgan's case.

The parade went off without a hitch. No assassination attempt, no terrorist attacks, no disruptions or protests, just a nice parade. I'm sure that when I meet with Snell to finalize Joe's release, he'll hint at what a wonderful job his FBI guys did in stopping the terrorist attacks. I know there's no use in asking for any details, because whenever anyone in government doesn't want to explain something, it becomes 'classified' information – which means that if he tells me, he'll have to kill me.

Before turning in I check the email and see that Mister Berland has forwarded Ralph Eaton's Notice of Petition to Administer Estate. He's pushing to have the proceeds of his mother-in-law's Will turned over to him.

It's kind of late, but I don't think he'll mind, so I call Mister Berland and explain to him that as a beneficiary of the Will, Eaton contacted his mother-in-law's Representative, the family lawyer preparing the Will, and asked him to file a Petition for Probate of the Estate. Once that's done and gets published, anyone considered by the court to be what they call an 'interested person' who wants to contest the Will has a statutory four-month period of time to file

163

objections with the court. The most common ones are that the decedent wasn't of sound mind, or the Will wasn't executed in a manner required by law, or that the Will was made as a direct result of undue influence. Unfortunately, none of those common objections will do him any good, so if he wants to prevent his son-in-law from getting any money, he's going to have to show that his daughter died first in the accident.

This is an extremely grim situation. I'm forcing a man who lost his wife and daughter to re-live the tragedy over and over again by re-hashing their deaths in an attempt to prove that he lost his daughter first, and then his wife. I don't like this part of practicing law, and now feel justified in never having taken the courses in law school that would have led me into conflicts like this on a regular basis.

I inform him that we're currently working on the case and he'll be brought up to speed if and when our investigation turns anything up. In the meantime, I get the name and number of his family attorney, the person who prepared the Wills. I want to let him take the lead in this matter, because he obviously knows more about the probate procedure than I do.

Mister Berland agrees with my decision and we make plans to talk again soon, perhaps in his family lawyer's office. And now it's to bed for me.

After a good night's sleep, I call Socrates Gutsue, the Berland family attorney, and inform him that Mister Berland would like to stop Ralph Eaton from getting half of the Berland assets.

He sympathizes with Mister Berland's wishes and informs me that according to our Probate Code, if Mister Berland wants to contest the Will, he must file his objection with the court and serve it on the other interested parties, so that a response can be filed and a hearing set.

I call Mister Berland and let him know that we will be filing the proper notice on his behalf, but there's no guarantee our investigation will support it at the hearing. He decides to take the risk and offers to send me a retainer check. Our office manager files the paperwork, and the forces are now in motion. I certainly hope that Victor can come up with some results, because if he doesn't, I'll be sitting there in that hearing with egg on my face, and that's not a good position for someone like me with high cholesterol to be in.

Next on my list of things to do is using the 'get out of jail' card that Snell offered me for Joe Morgan, so I call his office and his assistant relays the message to me. "Mister Sharp, Special Agent Snell has kept his word to you. Your client, Mister Joseph Morgan, will be cut loose this afternoon and we've notified the District Attorney's office of his pending release. They'll be sending two officers and transport, so the prisoner will be released to their custody."

Well, I guess that about all the freedom that Joe will have today is a brief ride down the street, from the Federal can to the County can. I'll have to get together with Myra's office to arrange for a bail hearing.

At this point I still can't connect Eaton with the death of his wife, so my entire argument against him collecting from her Will depends on Victor's showing that Nancy died before her mother did. Other than that, the only way to stop him from inheriting millions of dollars is to prove to the court that Eaton was involved in her death. The courts don't look favorably upon people who expect to inherit money from decedents who they had helped to become deceased, and as far as the State of California is concerned, I can't expect the Probate Court to suspect someone of complicity in murder while another court in the same County is holding another person for the same crime. This is a troubling situation.

Myra agrees to a meeting with me. I have a hearing coming up soon in Probate Court, so I get right to the point.

"Here's the way it is. We both know that you're weak in the motive department on my guy, so please consider this. The victim's husband stands to collect at least a million on her life insurance policy and another two million from her will. Now that's motive, so if you want a direction to look in, that's it.

"The husband also works at the same dealership as my client, and he was the general manager, with complete access to all service areas and all personnel. So if you want means, that's it.

"The husband also has one of the only full sets of keys to the dealership, which means that any vehicle left overnight for service is accessible to him – and each one of those three exploding Suburbans had been left overnight for service before they exploded. The dealership gives free loan cars, so people don't mind leaving their vehicles. So if you want opportunity, that's it.

"I'm not a trained prosecutor like you, but if you want a suspect who meets the three tests of means, motive, and opportunity, I'm giving you one on a silver platter.

"And if that's not good enough for you, then I'm sure it will be for a jury, because with the scenario I can propose to them, I've got no reasonable doubt about Eaton's being involved."

Myra takes it all in. She's not arguing with me yet, which is a good sign.

"Peter, you've got some good points about Mister Eaton, but you left out one minor item that we prosecutors like to have when we take a murder case to court, and it's called evidence. With all your eloquence, I haven't heard anything but an interesting theory that might even be true.

"On the other hand, we do have a person in custody who also had the means and the opportunity. He worked on all three of those vehicles and had a falling out with two of the owners. Now that might not be the strongest case in the world, but it's a lot stronger than the one you've built against your 'plan B' guy, the husband."

Damn, she's good. I've got to keep trying.

"Fine, you've got a suspect in custody, but having a patsy in the tank is a far cry from getting a conviction. We've already got an explosive expert to testify to the fact that the stuff they found at my client's house were just the mechanisms for a fireworks display, and I've got another witness who'll come in and testify that his firm hired Joe to make that device. I've also got our friend from West L.A. who'll come in and dazzle the jury with his FBI wardrobe and agree with my explosive expert.

"I know you've got nobody else to hang the murder rap on yet, but at least be reasonable with the bail. All he's really guilty of is some larceny from the manufacturer for okaying those unwarranted repairs, and when I get the owners on the stand, they'll probably testify that the only reason they suggested that Joe was upset at their not wanting to go ahead with the bribe scheme was because they were being brow-beaten by your aggressive investigators – and without that, you've got no motive at all, and no case."

Myra's not a mad-dog prosecutor. She always had a sense of fairness. My best shot is to give her a replacement suspect.

"Here's the deal. You tell your calendar deputy not to object to a reasonable bail of less than ten G's and I'll have my guy surrender his passport. This way, he'll be able to help me get the goods on Eaton. He serviced those vehicles before the explosions. Two of them were towed back to him after the explosions. He's been servicing them since the day they were brand new. If anyone can look at the one that went off of Mulholland and tell us what really happened, it's Joe Morgan, and we both need him on the street to help us.

"Tell you what. I'm not playing captain crime-buster any more. All the information our investigation turns up will be turned directly over to you. When we finish putting everything together, I'll even have Jack B. drive you to the courthouse steps in the Hummer so you can make your victory speech in front of the cameras. You'll be this County's District Attorney for Life, until you run for Governor. C'mon… Whatta ya say?"

Something must have worked, because tomorrow morning I'll be meeting the guy from Fradkin Bail Bonds in the courtroom and Joe Morgan will be walking out the door with me. I don't know if they'll be letting him walk back into the door of the dealership, but that's another problem. I try to limit my work to only one miracle a day.

11

Chicago can be hot in the summertime. Even more stifling is the humidity, and this Indian summer Monday in late September is no different. Being a low middle-class neighborhood in the northwest part of town called Albany Park, air conditioning is an unaffordable luxury. All the windows of the apartments in the court buildings on north Kedzie Avenue are open, so you don't have to be inside to hear the debate, especially since the debate is being broadcast internationally from a CBS studio in Chicago.

Howard K. Smith is the moderator, and probably every radio and television set in the country is tuned in to the same multi-cast, so even if you're walking on the street you can hear Mr. Smith begin.

"Good evening. The television and radio stations of the United States and their affiliated stations are proud to provide facilities for a discussion of issues in the current political campaign by the two major candidates for the presidency.

"The candidates need no introduction. The Republican candidate, Vice President Richard M. Nixon, and the Democratic candidate, Senator John F. Kennedy."

The adults are glued to their sets. This debate even attracts the attention of teen-agers, but three pre-teens in particular aren't very interested. They are little Ralph Eaton and his two buddies Alan

Rosenbaum and Marv Kupchic, who are too busy playing ball around the corner on Argyle Street at River Park, to pay attention to some stupid politicians.

These three close friends missed this first debate in 1961 and couldn't care less who was President, because their only interests at that time were baseball, and those two wonderful bumps under their classmate Shirley Morris' sweater.

Ralph, Alan, and Marv were the three musketeers. They all lived in the same court building, a three-story, 26-apartment building on the west side of the street, halfway between Ainslie and Argyle. They all got their social security cards together, with consecutive numbers. They went to Hibbard Elementary School and later attended Von Steuben High School, from which one of them would graduate – and they all loved cars.

Ralph was the only one who could keep out of trouble long enough to finish high school – the other two were thrown out for various reasons, including skipping classes and general disobedience. Their parents finally succeeded in buying them diplomas from some private high school downtown called 'Central Y,' where they actually attended a few classes, along with other miscreants from high schools all over the city who fashioned themselves after their 'Rebel Without A Cause' movie idols James Dean, Sal Mineo, and Corey Allen. They looked upon school as a 'Blackboard Jungle,' much like the stars of that movie, Vic Morrow and Sidney Portier did.

Alan's father ran the used car lot at Z. Frank Chevrolet on North Western Avenue, and when the old man wasn't on a binge with his friends, he would let the kid work there as a lot-boy. If Alan ever were to have a future doing anything, it would have to be in something to do with automobiles. He loved cars, especially the ones from General Motors, the company that pioneered those huge obscene fins sticking up out of rear fenders that first appeared on the 1948 Cadillacs.

Alan and Marv had a grand time stealing hubcaps off of parked cars and selling them to the used car lots up and down Western Avenue, Chicago's longest street, and home to more auto dealerships than any other street in the country.

In spite of several arrests and probation sentences, they continued their criminal behavior and graduated to stealing cars. There was no device like the *club* in those days, so cars were easy to snatch, especially after Alan stole some master keys from the dealership where his father worked and had copies made. This gave the two young men access to every General Motors vehicle in the greater Chicago area, and they capitalized on it by keeping several 'chop shops' supplied with a steady supply of 'donor' vehicles. Not being bogged down with the responsibility of several years of attending high school gave them the time to perfect their street skills.

By the time they were all nineteen years old, it was almost 1975 and the United States was involved in Viet Nam, fighting a war in which 58,168 young soldiers lost their lives, 153,303 were wounded, and almost 2,500 are still listed as missing in action.

Marv and Alan were not allowed to enlist because of their extensive criminal records as juveniles, but Ralph Eaton was accepted, and served his country admirably.

The only reason that their criminal enterprises ceased operating was the new job offer that Marv's father accepted somewhere in the Southeast. Alan, now without his close friends, decided that living with his alcoholic father and promiscuous mother was too much of a distraction from other more profitable pursuits, so he 'borrowed' one of the trade-ins from Z. Frank's used card lot and decided to try another state for a while.

Unfortunately, his criminal past kept him from getting any job that required fingerprinting for a license, so real estate, insurance, bail bonds, security guard, or car sales was out of the question. He did, however, have excellent skills as a mechanic. He could take apart and re-assemble any model Chevrolet blindfolded.

There was no email in those days, but Alan and Marv still managed to keep in touch by what we now call 'snail' mail. Alan noticed that Marv's letters were always written in pencil, with a Post Office Box as a return address, but he didn't really think much about it. They both lost touch with Ralph Eaton, who became a legitimate war hero and was definitely now out of their league.

The years passed by. Correspondence between Alan and Marv dwindled to only once or twice a year, but still kept up for many years to follow.

12

A District Attorney messenger just delivered some witness statements from the people who will be testifying against Joe Morgan at his trial. Each one of them admits to having paid anywhere from twenty to one hundred dollars for each unauthorized warranty repair to a vehicle.

Way down at the bottom of the last report is an investigator's note scribbled in the margin mentioning that the witnesses are prepared to bring into court proof of each payment that they made to have the repairs done.

What does that mean? Was Joe stupid enough to take their checks? I don't want to bring any unnecessary attention to this little detail, so I assign Jack B. the task of contacting each of these witnesses and making photocopies of whatever they claim to be proof of payment to Joe.

While waiting for Jack to round up those copies, I've made an appointment to pick up Joe and bring him with me to where the wrecked Suburban is, so that he can check out my information about the right front brake caliper. I offer to take him to his apartment first so that he can rest up for a while, but he insists on getting right to the investigation. He wants very much to completely clear his name, and I don't blame him.

He looks pretty good for having spent some time in custody. He credits it all to his Seal training. When we get to the police impound garage, the same surly tattooed gate attendant who directed me to Stuart's Camry is there to greet us with a frown. After making us sit on a couple of grimy chairs for about fifteen minutes while he calls someone at another location, he grudgingly buzzes us through to the large out-door vehicle storage area.

Impounded vehicles that are subjects of criminal investigation are stored in an indoor 'evidence' garage, which is kept locked at all times. Smiley opens the locked door for us and we go inside. There are only two other vehicles in the garage, both probably recovered stolens. I remind myself to mention this fact to Stuart so that he can start keeping track of local police auctions.

The Suburban is on an alignment rack. It would be a lot easier if it was all the way up on a hoist, but the rack is okay because we see what Joe refers to as a 'creeper' nearby. I know what he means when I see him go over to get the thing. It's like a little furniture dolly with wheels that a mechanic can lie on and roll himself under a vehicle, for a look at the car's bottom.

Joe doesn't waste any time. Using the flashlight that he asked me to bring in from my glove compartment, he lies down on the creeper, rolls himself under the Suburban and starts investigating whatever there is to investigate down there.

After a few minutes of poking around he gets up and tells me that in order to do a more thorough job he'll need some tools from his cabinet at the dealership. I'll have to take his word for it, because I still don't even understand what a caliper is.

When we pull into the dealership, it looks like old home week with a hero returning from the war. Obviously not one person in the whole place believed that Joe had anything to do with those explosions, and he's tremendously well liked by everyone there. We don't see Eaton around, but that's no surprise. He probably knew that we'd be coming by today so he made himself scarce.

Our appearance is during the middle of everyone's lunch break, so Joe is having a nice time making the rounds and saying hello to all his fellow employees. While he was gone his service bay was closed, so he has to use his security key to unlock the roll-down gate and lift it up in order to enter the bay. It was a clean workspace when he left it, and it stayed that way.

Like most journeymen mechanics, he has a six-foot high red metal tool cabinet on wheels, with plenty of different sized drawers. I don't know too much about tools, but judging from the size of that cabinet, I'd bet that he has whatever could possibly be needed for just about any vehicle repair.

Joe looks a little confused at first and has to open several drawers before he finds what he needs. I'm curious about this.

"What's the matter Joe, forget where you put some things?"

"Naw, I don't do brake work in my bay. We have a separate department on the other side of the lot that does alignment, brakes, shocks, mufflers, and stuff like that. I haven't used my brake-pulling tools in a long time, and for some reason they're not in the drawer I thought they were in."

He fumbles through another couple of drawers and finally locates the tool he was looking for. Suddenly, out of pure reflex action, I shout out to him. "Wait, Joe, don't touch it."

He's got good reflexes. His military training kicked in to obey my command and he doesn't touch the tool.

"Sorry about that Joe, but remember what we were talking about? Well, if you didn't do anything to those vehicles, then it's a good possibility that after hours someone else did. If that's true, then we've got to get that tool dusted it for prints."

"That's a good idea Mister Sharp, but you know what grease does... it destroys a hard surface's ability to accept a print."

"Yeah Joe, I know that, but you told me that you haven't used that tool in quite some time, so if you've haven't done much work with it, maybe we can get lucky and it's in a like-new condition without much grease on it."

We take that tool and some of the others that might have possibly been used to sabotage a brake system and put them into a plastic souvenir bag we borrow from the dealership's gift shop. I'll have Jack B. take the bag out to Victor's place.

I purposely avoid discussing the note that the D.A.'s investigator made about proof of payments to Joe. No sense in asking questions I don't know some answers to. I want to be able to know the facts, so that when we start to discuss the matter I'll be able to find out once and for all whether or not Joe's been lying to me. I'd rather go along with the Ronald Reagan slogan of 'trust, but verify.'

Joe and I both agree that it would be best for him to lock up his service bay and go home to wait for some word from the dealership as to the status of his employment there. That Suburban will still be available for Joe to inspect next week. As for Joe's job, I don't think that Eaton will want him to stay, because that might look too much like Joe's innocent of the murders, and he's too convenient a suspect to let off the hook right now – at least until the insurance and estate monies come in for Eaton, at which time he probably won't care about much. He'll be long gone and far away.

After several days of nothing happening, Mister Berland's family attorney Socrates Gutsue calls to let me know that the Probate Court has set a hearing date for the objection he filed on Berland's behalf. This means that if we can't give the court some reason not to go ahead, they will accept Mrs. Berland's Will into probate and start the process that will make Ralph Eaton a multi-millionaire.

The next phone call that comes in is from Victor.

"Peter, I've got news for you. Do you want to hear the bad news or the bad news?"

"I get the idea Victor… let's get it over with. What've you got?"

"First, I haven't been able to figure out who died first - Nancy Eaton or her mother. Next, I did manage to get some prints off of one of your client's brake tools, but the locals have nothing to match it in the California database. I've sent it to the Feds, but that takes longer, so we'll have to wait a while, until AFIS sends an answer. And last but certainly not least, I've been subpoenaed to testify at the Probate Court's Will Contest Hearing later this week."

"C'mon Victor, they can't be serious about that. If you don't know enough to advise me, what can they think you'll be able to tell them?"

"I don't know either, Pete, but the papers they served on me require that I bring all the photos along with me to the hearing, so maybe there's something there I haven't noticed yet."

This is a fine mess. Not only do I have nothing at all to use in support of Mister Berland's objection to the probate proceeding, my only possible witness has been ordered to come in and testify against us. I make arrangements to meet Victor at the courthouse an hour before the hearing and start to prepare myself mentally for an embarrassing loss. I warned Mister Berland that we might not stand a chance.

There's a knock on the hull. Jack B. is here with copies of the medical records on Nancy Eaton and her mother. I call a friend of mine who used to practice internal medicine and after about thirty minutes of reading a foreign language to him he tells me that Nancy Eaton had a heart condition resulting in an irregular heartbeat. I don't know if it helps me, but it's all I've got.

At the Probate hearing I introduce myself to the dapper Socrates Gutsue, Berland's family lawyer. He's been handling the Berland personal and business affairs for the past thirty years and also prepared both of their Wills. He asks me what we have to work with on the objection, and I sheepishly confess that we haven't been able to come up with anything substantial.

"Well Mister Sharp, should we just call this whole objection hearing off, or do you want to go in there and give it a shot?"

I tell Socrates I've never won a card game that I didn't play in, so we all enter the courtroom together and see Ralph Eaton with his lawyer already seated at their respective places behind the counsel table. He's retained an attorney named Paul Larkin, who I've been up against in the past. He's a first class schmuck. They both look confident, and I don't blame them. As a matter of courtesy I go over and say hello to them, but there is no shaking of hands. Before returning to our side of the courtroom, I take the opportunity to ask Larkin one question. "Why did you subpoena Victor Gutierrez to come in today? Do you think he has some important information that will show which one of them died first?"

Larkin smirks as he answers me. "Not really, Sharp, I know he has nothing that can help you, so I wanted to make sure he was here to help you make a fool out of yourself."

Great. That's the kind of moral support I really need before starting a hearing that's a guaranteed dead-bang loser. It also proves the old saying about birds of a feather. A jerk like Eaton found an attorney he could identify with.

Being an informal hearing, there is no armed bailiff to call the court to order, and rightfully so, because we're the only ones in the room. The judge walks in, steps up and sits down behind the bench. The court file has already been placed in front of him, so he calmly looks up and starts the proceeding.

"In the matter of the Will of one deceased Estelle Berland, the file indicates that there has been an objection filed concerning the time of death. The moving party contends that Estelle Berland's primary beneficiary, her daughter Nancy Eaton, pre-deceased her, therefore requiring that portion of her estate intended for the daughter instead to be re-directed to her alternate beneficiary, her husband.

"Mister Gutsue, you're the attorney of record for the moving party. You've appeared before me many times and I'm sure you know the way it works. It's your objection, so it's your burden of proof. Let's hear what you've got."

"Thank you Your Honor. At this time I'd like to have attorney Peter Sharp take over the presentation of evidence. He is our special co-counsel in this matter."

This is the moment every lawyer dreads... being called on in open court to say something when you have absolutely nothing to say. And not only do I know I have nothing to say, opposing counsel knows it too. Caving now would let the court know that we've wasted its time with a frivolous objection, and that's the type of insult no member of the bar wants to give to any judge.

I stand up and start talking. Nothing special, but I must be talking because I hear some words coming out of my mouth, and there's no one else standing up but me. The only chance I have is to put Victor on the stand and hope that I can get him to admit that it's possible that the daughter predeceased the mother. That's not going to cut it in this court and I know it, but it's all I've got.

Victor takes the witness stand and is sworn in. He looks relaxed. He should look relaxed. He's got nothing to lose today because he gets paid his seven-hundred-fifty-dollar witness fee whether he talks or not. I might as well make him work a little for it, so I start in with the usual questions. We cover every word in the police accident investigation reports, and I concentrate on the fact that the daughter was thrown clear of the car while the mother stayed in it all the way down the hill. My only hope is to try and get the judge to believe that because the daughter was thrown clear of the car, she probably died instantly, leaving the mother alive in the car for the rest of the way down the hill.

Naturally, Larkin is up and down like a jack-in-the-box, objecting to every question I ask Victor. The judge probably feels a little sorry for me fighting such a losing battle, but if asked, he would have to admit that I'm at least giving it my all.

Victor had some enlargements made of the accident scene photos, and one of them is propped up on an exhibit easel near the judge's bench. As I'm questioning Victor, I keep looking at it and see that it's a shot of the car after it came to rest. The front windshield has been shattered inward, probably as the result of hitting a tree branch on the way down the hill. Mrs. Berland is still in the vehicle and the photo shows her covered with broken glass and her own blood. This must be a terribly uncomfortable thing for Mister Berland, sitting there directly in front of these grim pictures showing his dead wife and daughter. The old man's holding up pretty well though, and I give him credit for that.

On the other hand, Ralph Eaton seems more interested in whispering strategy into his lawyer's ear. He doesn't seem the slight bit bothered by the picture of his wife lying on top of a boulder.

We show another enlargement of the Suburban's interior, after Mrs. Eaton's bloody body was removed. I can see that both front airbags had been deployed and deflated. That probably happened when the vehicle crashed through the road's guardrail and started its descent.

Something's wrong with these pictures. It's all over the photographs and hiding in plain sight. It's the blood. Suddenly I feel like there's a way to go here. I brought my whole file along and it includes the doctor's report about Nancy Eaton's heart trouble, so I ask Victor if it's possible that Nancy died of a heart failure while her mother was still riding down the hill.

As expected, Larkin is up out of his seat.

"We strenuously object to this line of questioning to this witness. He's not a medical doctor and can't possibly qualify to testify as an expert as to any live person's health condition."

The judge would like to hear more of my argument, but in order for him to do that he must first rule on this objection to Victor's testimony. I see the judge looking down at me over his glasses with an expression of curiosity on his face.

"Your Honor, we are not attempting to qualify Mister Gutierrez as an expert medical witness. He is here today as the result of being subpoenaed by Mister Larkin, so his testimony should not be treated so lightly. Furthermore, while not a licensed physician, he has taught autopsy science and procedure to countless medical students and coroners' staff throughout the United States, and his expert opinion as to cause of death is highly respected by bench and bar alike.

"The question we are now putting to him is not merely to seek an opinion of her health while alive, but to ask him to state whether or not in his many years of doing post mortem examinations he has ever seen a person with the type of medical condition Nancy Eaton had, die instantly in an automobile accident."

Larkin won't let go. He jumps up again and starts to shout more objections, trying to stop Victor from answering my question. It worked. Contrary to public opinion, judges are human too, and subject to having just as much curiosity as the rest of us. Experience has taught me that if you can get a judge involved in what you're trying to bring out in court, he's more likely to be influenced by his own curiosity, and that's what probably happened here. The judge is curious to see where I'm going with my questioning, so he tells Larkin to sit down, because he won't sustain the objection. Victor is allowed to answer my question and he does by telling us that it is possible that Nancy Eaton died instantly, prior to her mother's death.

Larkin correctly argues that 'possible' isn't good enough here. He points out that the burden of proof is on us to establish that Nancy died first by at least a preponderance of the evidence, and not just by a mere possibility. The judge agrees with him. I feel a lot better already. This hearing started out with me not standing a chance in hell, and now I feel like I'm at least back in the game. I'll probably lose anyway, but at least I'm back in the game.

My next line of questioning to Victor is quite simple to follow, and almost objection proof.

"Mister Gutierrez, you perform autopsies on dead bodies, is that correct?"

"Yes, Mister Sharp. The State doesn't like us to perform autopsies on people until they're actually dead."

Victor knows I'm making him work for his money, so I don't blame him for having a little fun with me.

"Mister Gutierrez, would you please tell the court if it is possible for a dead body to gush blood?"

Victor knows where I'm going with this and so does Larkin, but there's nothing he can do about it.

Victor answers as expected, that dead bodies don't gush blood. This leads to my next series of question regarding the photos of the smashed window and Estelle Berland covered with blood. The logical conclusion that the judge should reach is that she was alive while the car was rolling down the hill.

This is a big victory, because we have just established that she didn't die instantly. It doesn't mean that she died before or after her daughter, it only means that she didn't die instantly, and that's half the battle.

My next series of questions establishes where Nancy Eaton's body was found and how close to the roadway it was. This is an attempt to establish the fact that she was tossed free of the car before it started it's descent down the hill.

We bring up the picture of Nancy Eaton lying on top of the boulder. There is no blood to be seen. My contention is that she was dead when she hit the boulder and therefore must have been dead when being tossed from the vehicle.

I sum up my argument to the court by contending that the blood tells the tale - none on the daughter, plenty on the mother. Therefore, our entire objection is that the daughter died instantly from heart failure when the car hit the guardrail and the airbags deployed. She was then thrown from the car and landed on a large boulder, not shedding a drop of blood. Her mother was still alive and bleeding during her trip down the hill. Pictures of the car after she was removed show a complete pattern of blood, indicating that she was alive and bleeding while the car was rolling down the hill. The daughter died first.

The judge doesn't make an instant ruling. Instead, he says he'll take the matter under submission, which means he'll think about it for a couple of weeks before sending us postcards with his decision. We fill out the postcards and leave the courtroom. On the way out, I make every effort to thank Eaton and attorney Larkin.

"Gentlemen, I couldn't do it without you. Thanks for forcing Victor to be here with his pictures."

Mister Berland and his attorney are both pleased with the way it went in court. I remind Socrates to tell Berland that it isn't over until it's over. He nods in acknowledgment and we all head for our respective parking spaces. I owe Jack B. another one for those medical reports.

On the way out of court, Victor calls me aside.

"By the way Peter, I got some results on those prints from the brake tool. There was a match."

"Really Victor, did the national database come through for you?"

"Better than that, Peter, I used another database – one that I'd almost forgotten about. I keep a file on every print I've ever lifted, so I tried matching the tool prints with that file. And whatta ya think? I found a match."

"Don't keep me guessing Vic, who's the bomber? We'd really like to find him."

"You already found him, Pete... he's Marv Kupchic, the stiff from Stuart's trunk."

13

I email a report to Indovine's office and his reply is encouraging. He's especially pleased that I sprung Joe Morgan, hoping that the dealership will also be cleared of any civil liability.

Unfortunately, it appears that Indovine's pleasure is pre-mature, because my caller ID display shows Joe Morgan's telephone number. I answer and say hello.

"Mister Sharp? This is Joe Morgan."

"Yes Joe, I know... what can I do for you today?"

"I'm going back to jail, Mister Sharp... they're here right now arresting me. The lady said it would be okay to make a quick phone call to you."

"Just keep cool, Joe. Remember what I told you last time: don't talk to anyone unless I'm there. You can give your statistics to the jailer when he books you, but otherwise, no conversation... and that goes for anyone you're in the holding tank or a cell with. Got it?"

"Yes sir Mister Sharp, I got it."

"Good. Now, would you please put that lady on the phone?"

"Do you want me to find out her name for you?"

"No, that's okay Joe, I've met her before."
Joe follows my instructions and hands Myra the
phone.

"Hello Petey, I'm sorry, but our office has
decided to pick your guy up. It's some new evidence
we've got."

"Myra, I know you have to do your job, and I
appreciate your letting him call me, but what could
you possibly know today that you didn't know last
week?"

"We've got a motive now, Pete, and as you
correctly pointed out before, that was our big weak
point."

"I'm coming to your office later today to talk
about this. If you've got some new evidence, I'm
entitled to know what it is, and in this case I'd like to
get it from you face to face, and not from this
evening's news broadcast."

We make an appointment to meet at her office
in an hour, and now fifty minutes later I'm sitting in
the outer waiting room. A clerk, who I remember
seeing at the L.L.B. luncheon that Patty Seymour
took me to, motions that it's okay to go into Myra's
office. I don't waste any time with small talk.

"Okay Miss Prosecutor, what've you got?"

"Well, here are two documents from the
public records of the State Fire Marshal and Division
of Industrial Safety that show your client's
applications for the licenses of Pyrotechnic Operator
and Explosive Blaster."

"Gee, why stop there. With a little more effort you could probably even find out that at one time he applied for a driver's license. What's the big deal with these application forms? We all know he's had military training in the use of explosives... hell, that's one of the reasons you arrested him in the first place. All these applications show is that he wants to do things legally. Are you telling me that you had a judge revoke his bail and re-arrested him because he applied for some licenses?"

"No Peter, it's more than that. First of all, he applied for these licenses several weeks prior to the first non-fatal Suburban explosion. Second, we have a witness that will testify to the fact that your client had a disagreement with one of the victims, Nancy Eaton. Third, we believe that as a result of that disagreement, she notified both licensing boards that she would object to the granting of the licenses. Put all that together and you've got a little thing that we call motive."

"And exactly what do you have to substantiate your allegation that Nancy Eaton lodged a complaint with those agencies?"

"They've told our investigators that upon receipt of a subpoena from our office that they will produce the complaint letter their office received."

"That's wonderful. Are you listening to yourself talk? You just told me that an investigator heard from someone else that he could get a letter purportedly sent by the deceased victim. I don't know what the record is for how many rules of evidence you can sidestep at one time, but I'm going to nominate you for it.

"Myra, don't you see? What you've got is a textbook example of a frame-up, and I know exactly who is behind it... the dealership's general manager, Mister Ralph Eaton. I don't know how he did it, but believe me... he's behind this whole mess. He made all three of those vehicles explode, he killed his wife and mother-in-law, he's in line to collect over three million dollars from insurance and probate, and he planned the whole frame job on Joe Morgan.

"I don't have the evidence yet, but I'm going to get it. There've been several times in the past when I warned you not to go ahead with matters... that you'd be making a fool out of yourself. And, if you remember correctly, I was right. Well, sweetheart, this is another one of those times."

She's sitting there like a pro and taking my ranting without fighting back. I know in my heart that she has a feeling I might be right. I don't want to hear what she's got to say, so I storm out of the office and note that everyone is looking at me as I leave. I guess I was shouting a little louder than usual and it must have been a wonderful show. I hope they enjoyed it.

Boy, I am steamed, and it must show, because as I drive west on Venice Boulevard back towards the Marina, other drivers are getting out of the way. If there's one thing you don't want to do, it's piss off a guy driving a large Hummer, especially if you're driving a sub-compact car and your eye level is even with my front bumper.

She's got a lot of nerve doing this, because her case wouldn't be hurt at all by leaving him out on bail. He's not a danger to himself or anyone else, and he's certainly not a flight risk. Can she be seriously thinking that he'd kill someone because of a complaint for some stinking license? That's ridiculous. I've seen too many people in positions like her make decisions for political reasons that have nothing to do with a case, and a prime example was that jerk-off who had the job as D.A. before she got it. I sure hope that Joe's being a Muslim had nothing to do with her decision, because if it did, I'm going to make sure that it comes back and bites her in the ass before this case is over.

It's still light out when I get back to the boat. I need a drink to calm down. Maybe I'll go over to Laverne's boat for a backrub and a box of wine. That'll calm me down. I hear the familiar pitter-patter of huge paws. It's dogmail time, and I'm pleased to see that the kid is following my request to tuck the message in his collar, because it stays a lot dryer that way. It's not a message from the kid. Damn! It's a note from Socrates Gutsue. He spoke to the clerk at the Probate Court and found out that the judge denied our objection and that Mrs. Berland's will is being accepted for probate.

How can this be? Is that judge nuts or something? I made a good case in there that the daughter died first. Didn't he understand it? This is probably another case of a lawyer who was too stupid to make it in private practice so he borrowed some money from his family, made a contribution to the right campaign fund, and bought himself a judgeship. If he had half a brain he would have taken that fifty grand and bought himself a job as a maitre'd in some Las Vegas hotel. The health benefits are probably the same, but the tips are probably twice as much as a judge makes, and almost tax-free. And that doesn't even take into consideration the extra bonus of the proximity to those leggy showgirls.

The thought of showgirls has now left my brain and I'm back to realizing that my day has been ruined. Thanks to Ralph Eaton, my professional life has just dived into the dumper. His frame-up of Joe is working, his penalty-free murder of two people is working, his inheritance is working, and his insurance claim is working. What am I doing wrong? How can I stop this guy? Is he that much smarter than me?

From this moment on I intend to devote full time to bringing this guy down. The kid has been listening to me ranting and raving in anger at my last two unfortunate callers, Socrates Gutsue and Mister Berland. She has been peeking out of her stateroom door, probably to see if I turn green when I get mad. I call Jack B. and send him to the District Attorney's office for a copy of the first recorded anonymous tip that was phoned in to them about Joe Morgan. I want to hear that voice and find out if it matches up with anyone else we might know. If my hunch is right, it'll be Ralph Eaton's voice.

His next job is to find out everything he can about Ralph Eaton's background. I want to know more about this guy, because he' a real piece of work.

The phone rings. It's Victor at the autopsy store. He's got some results on the fingerprints he ran from the brake tools in Joe's service bay and Stuart's trunk – the one the body was in.

There's a coincidence that shows in the results. They're both small-time crooks with similar records that date back thirty years in Chicago, Illinois. This is interesting, because investigators love to find patterns. These two guys must have known each other. Both from the same town, both with similar records, and now one has killed the other and somehow managed to get him into Stuart's trunk.

The other interesting thing is that one of them was handling Joe's tools. I call Jack B. and tell him to look very deeply into whether or not Ralph Eaton has ever been in Chicago – especially thirty years ago. Eaton and the other two are all about the same age, so I'm hoping we can tie them together, because if we can, it will mean that Eaton may have hired one to kill the other.

I call Mister Berland. Most of our conversation is my apologizing about my show of anger during our recent conversation earlier today, and the rest of it is to ask only one question. "During the time that Eaton was married to your daughter, are you aware of any trips for business or pleasure that both of them or he alone may have taken out of the country?"

Berland thinks about it for a few seconds and then tells me that he thinks the dealership sent Eaton to Taiwan a few years back, to investigate the possibility of making some automobile accessories there.

I'm glad to hear that, because it means that he must have applied for a passport, and that requires a birth certificate that shows exactly when and where you were born. I tell Jack B. to do whatever it takes to get us a copy of that passport application, and if the word 'Illinois' appears anywhere on it, that he should pack his bags, because he'll be on a flight to O'Hare International Airport in Chicago.

Two days have gone by and Jack B. hasn't got Eaton's passport application info yet. He tells me that it might be coming to him later today.

There's a knock on the hull. I look over the rail, but it's no one I recognize. I ask the guy what he wants, and I'm told that it's a special delivery for attorney Peter Sharp. I reach down, take the envelope out of his hand, and open it up to see that I've just been served with a Summons and Complaint. Ralph Eaton is suing me for five million dollars, claiming that I defamed him by making an accusation to the authorities that he is guilty of murder. I guess that my shouting in Myra's office let everyone on the floor know my suspicions about Eaton. He probably pumped some information out of one of the secretaries by promising some repairs on her car and got the details of my tirade.

When a person gets served with a lawsuit, the law allows a certain amount of days to file an official

'Answer' with the court, but it's almost a given that a first extension of another thirty days or so will be granted if the defense attorney calls the plaintiff's attorney and asks for it. Paul Larkin is representing Eaton on this matter too, and I don't want to creep myself out by hearing his voice on the phone, so I send an email to his office asking for the courtesy of one thirty-day extension to file my Answer.

My answer comes back by email. "Mister Sharp, we have discussed this matter with our client and he wishes to proceed with the case as expeditiously as possible, so we regret to inform you that your request for an extension is denied. Please file your Answer in the statutory period of time or we will be seeking a default judgment."

What an asshole. I give the paperwork to our office manager to have a standard denial Answer prepared and filed with the court by mail. There's only one good thing about this new lawsuit. In a criminal case, a person doesn't have to testify at all, but in a civil case, the plaintiff must testify, if requested. This means that I'll get a crack at this schmuck while he's under oath in a deposition, and if I can use my brain properly, I may even get enough evidence to put him away.

Once a lawsuit is filed, either side has the right to what is referred to as 'civil discovery,' which can be written questions or an oral 'deposition.' All questions must be answered under penalty of perjury unless they're justifiably objectionable or completely not related to any issue involved in the case.

In all my years of practice, I've never seen a set of written Interrogatories that didn't start out requesting the basic statistics like birth date, birthplace, residential, educational, and employment history. It can take over a month to get the Interrogs drawn up, served and receive the answers, so we have some time to find if there are any skeletons in Eaton's closet and prepare some nice questions that will give him enough rope to hang himself in a deposition or trial.

The office is being instructed to include with our Answer a Statutory Offer of Settlement in the sum of one dollar. That may not sound too significant, but I seem to remember some California case law that says if a Statutory Offer is refused and the person making the offer winds up with a more favorable disposition of the case, then the party who turned down the offer is responsible for the other party's legal fees. Nothing would make me happier than to win this non-case and have Eaton and Larkin be forced by the court to pay Suzi's hourly rate for the work she puts in on it.

I call Vaughn, my explosives expert. The questions I have for him concern the application for those two licenses that Joe wanted as a pyrotechnic operator and explosive blaster. As expected, Vaughn has both of those licenses. We talk about what type of background an applicant must have, how Joe's military training qualifies him as a licensee, what exactly can be done to earn a living with each of the licenses, and the procedure of responding to complaints from third persons that might be presented during the license investigation process.

Vaughn doesn't disappoint me. From the information he provides me with, I now know that with those licenses Joe would be able to do just about any task that Mrs. Berland wanted to hire him for, from being a mere fireworks guy, to working with Berland's other division that demolishes buildings and helps blast the way for tunnel and freeway routes. He also tells me that just about the only thing that would stop the licenses from going through would be a felony conviction or pending felony charges.

This means that if it really was Nancy Eaton who sent in that complaint letter, it would have been done while she was alive, so there were no felony charges to talk about. The only other thing she might have known about was the alleged bribery scheme for warranty repairs, and Vaughn doubts if an accusation like that, even if proved to be true, would stop them from licensing Joe as an official 'powder man.'

I thought so. Not only did Eaton do everything I suspect him of doing, he must have also cooked up that phony complaint to the licensing boards, in an effort to manufacture some motive for my unsuspecting ex-wife District Attorney. But how the hell can I get her to believe me? I sure hope she doesn't fall flat on her face with this one. I do want to win, but would hate to do it at the expense of her reputation or career.

14

I t's time to have another talk with the witness that Myra has about Joe's alleged bribery scheme. Before getting into it I'd like to know a little more about some of those repairs. Jack B. has a full plate, but I convince him to make some room for a few other items before we find out if he's going to Chicago or not. I want him to get a computer printout from the dealership of every warranty repair authorized by Joe that was made on any vehicle owned by either of the two witnesses, and I then want him to take that information to the local General Motors factory representative to find out how much of the work done actually would have been kosher under the warranties.

Jack tells me that he plans to inform the factory rep that they're investigating charges of unauthorized warranty repairs having been made, and that if the rep cooperates, it might result in a nice refund check coming back from the dealership. Of course he'll tell the dealership the opposite, leading them to believe that they may be getting some money from their customers.

I think Jack's got the right cover stories to go with, so we give it a shot and he starts at the dealership. The printout is quite extensive, but Vaughn turns us on to an ex-cop from auto theft, and with his help we decipher the data. Now Jack has enough ammo to talk to the rep without making a fool out of himself.

After we get more answers we'll be in a much better position to confront the Suburban owner-witnesses and also ask Joe some pointed questions. As much as I believe in his innocence on the murder charges, I still can't forget the rule that all clients will lie to you. They may not be intentionally wanting to deceive or mislead you, but in their avid attempt to get you on their side to be a strong advocate, there's too much of a chance for their autonomic exaggeration hormones to kick in.

While Jack is running himself ragged with the recent assignments, I sit back and start to compose some harmless looking questions for the written Interrogatories that will be sent to Larkin's office for Eaton to answer. Along with the questions will be a polite note from me telling them that we'll be expecting the answers in a timely fashion and that no extensions will be granted. What goes around comes around.

I'll probably be using some boilerplate questions out of the law books that give examples of what questions to ask for each type of case, but the only answers I'll be really interested in seeing are the statistical ones. To make them look especially easy, I construct long, probing and probably objectionable questions for the remainder of the Interrogs. I want them to answer the easy ones without even thinking about it so that they can waste all their efforts fighting off answering the rest of the questions that I don't even care about. This shouldn't be much harder than fooling a little kid by making some fancy motions with one hand and then pulling a quarter out of his ear with the other hand.

It's amazing how fast time flies by when you're having fun, and designing tortuous questions for Eaton to answer is definitely fun, especially when I don't care what the answers to ninety-nine percent of them are.

Two days have gone by and the Interrogs are ready to be sent to Larkin's office. Jack B. finally got the information from Eaton's passport application. He wasn't able to get a copy, but he was successful in learning that the birthplace was indeed Chicago, at the Michael Reese Hospital. I tell him to get packed. He's flying to Chicago the day after tomorrow and I'll arrange to have either Olive or Vinnie take him to the airport. He requests Vinnie. The kid has some leads for him to follow up there on the two thugs we got prints from, but most of Jack's work will be talking to people who knew them both, and doing a background investigation on everyone involved.

The rep from General Motors calls and tells us that all repairs made to the two owners' vehicles we questioned him about were within warranty limits. He explains that even though a dealership might be justified in denying the service in quite a few of those instances, it's the dealership's call on whether or not to treat them as warranty repairs, and in all cases the factory will usually back them up –

especially when it's a major dealership like the one we're talking about here.

Interesting. All the repairs made to those owners' vehicles actually qualified as warranty service, notwithstanding the fact that they were 'iffy' at most. This means that technically, there couldn't have been a bribe for unauthorized repairs to be performed, because all that the owners received were things they were actually entitled to. So if their payments to Joe weren't bribes, then what the hell were they?

I've seen plenty of instances where you have to 'grease' someone's palm to get what you're entitled to - that's how good seats at a show in Vegas, a good and timely booth in a restaurant, preferred parking in a lot, and thousands of other things are obtained, but I don't really know how to classify Joe's situation. Was he receiving 'tips,' bribes, or gifts? Our office usually gives a Christmas gift to the mailman each year. Does that mean we're supposed to believe that without giving the gift, we wouldn't receive our mail each day? I think not. Now it's time to talk to these alleged bribery witnesses.

I purposely planned Jack's trip to Chicago for the day after tomorrow to give him a chance to interview the witnesses before he leaves.

He gets all his paperwork together and prepares a file on each customer, so that when he meets with them, they might possibly be under the impression that he's working with the District Attorney's office. I give him specific orders to say nothing to make the witnesses think he's with the D.A., but at the same time to not dispel their mistaken beliefs if they don't ask him to.

Jack does a thorough job. He meets with each of the owners and lays the file out for them, making sure to let them know that in no way are they in any danger of getting in trouble, because it's the defendant he's after. They all swallow his line, because the cooperation is more than one hundred percent. One of the wives goes so far as to prepare a snack for him while he's there.

When he returns to the boat this evening for his report, he tells me the most amazing thing I've ever heard in a bribery investigation – the witnesses have proof of their payment, because they paid by check.

This means one of two things. Either Joe Morgan is the dumbest person on earth, or he didn't consider the payments as bribes. Jack didn't get copies of the cancelled checks but he did get a list of the dates they were made and the amounts, which were all the same. They were for twenty-five dollars each time. At least he's consistent. The last time Myra arrested him they got copies of his bank statements and found those deposits from Mrs. Berland that we now know were for preparing some fireworks displays. I received copies of his statements before his preliminary hearing, and when comparing them to the dates that the witnesses said they wrote their checks, I don't see the deposits. Like so many other people in this country, Joe's sole source of steady income was his paycheck, which was deposited directly to his bank account from the dealership. That deposit is the same every week, and shows up on his statement. If Joe deposited any other amounts, either when they were received or later on, they'd stick out on his bank records like a sore thumb. They aren't there. They don't appear anywhere. This may mean that he cashed the checks at the banks they were drawn on, but I doubt it. Those banks are only open during the time that Joe was busy in his service bay, and it's unlikely that he would drive all the way across town to cash a twenty-five dollar check in rush hour traffic, each time one came in.

I instruct the office to subpoena the witnesses' bank records and then I drive down to County Jail to visit with my client.

Joe is brought into the attorney visiting area and neither one of us looks very happy.

"Hello, Joe. How're you holding up?"

"About as well as can be expected. What brings you down here? Any news?"

"Yes Joe, as a matter of fact there is some news. My investigator interviewed the witnesses who claimed they bribed you to authorize warranty repairs to their vehicles, and they claim they paid you by check. We also made a computer run of all those alleged unauthorized warranty repairs and the GM factory rep says that they all could have legitimately been classified as authorized under the warranties. So what the hell's going on?"

"Nothing's going on. The repairs were authorized and would have been done whether they paid any money or not. It's not my fault if they felt compelled to make some small gifts every once in a while."

"That's bullshit, Joe. It's too coincidental that the only time they ever made what you call a gift is when they were having some service done to their car."

"Of course. What do you think, that they hang out with me in the service bay when they haven't got anything better to do? The only time I ever saw those people was when they came in for service."

"I'm not happy finding out that you're a petty thief, Joe."

"Don't give me that holier than thou crap. Do you always put as many stamps on a package that are required, or do you try to cheat an ounce or two? And how about your income tax? Is every cent you write off really a business expense, because if you screw around with that you're stealing from the United States Government, and that means from me, because my taxes have to make up for the slack that you honest do-gooders create with your creative accounting. Nobody's squeaky-clean Mister Sharp, so please don't come in here making any judgments. And as far as those witnesses of yours are concerned, you'd better do some more investigating, because you won't be able to prove I ever accepted a penny from them. Ever."

Suffice it to say that the interview doesn't end on a happy note. However, he did get my attention

210

with his remark about never receiving a penny from the witnesses. I'd better wait until their bank statements come in before I visit him again.

Jack gets lucky, because Vinnie does the airport driving for him. Olive's nails aren't dry enough to drive and she certainly doesn't want to ruin a manicure. Jack promises to call me as soon as he checks into his room at the Lincoln Arms in Skokie, Illinois. I know he'll be in room 2F, so it's probably at least on the second floor.

There's a knock on the hull. It's a messenger from the copy service that was sent to the witnesses' banks for their records. I tip him two dollars and wonder if it's a bribe or a gift, and if it makes any difference that he would have handed me the folder even if I didn't give him anything. While it's still fresh in my mind I dash off another email to a friend of mine who runs an Ethics Institute here in the Marina. It'll be interesting to see what his comments are on both Joe Morgan's actions and mine.

The package from the copy service contains bank statements and a list of the payees of each check. I give the stuff to our office manager, with instructions to find every twenty-five dollar check written to Joe Morgan. I'd also like to know if Joe reported these 'gifts' as income, because I know how he looks down upon tax cheats.

It takes less than an hour for my crack office staff to come up with some answers, which are sent to me in the form of a memo delivered by dogmail.

Each one of the owners did write checks for twenty-five dollars on the several dates that coincided with their auto repairs, but not one check was made payable to Joe Morgan. They were all written to the 'St. Mark's Catholic Church.'

Something doesn't compute here. An automobile warranty service mechanic does factory-authorized repairs to vehicles in a dealership, and the owners write checks to a Catholic Church on behalf of a Muslim. I must be missing something. This calls for a trip over to St. Mark's.

When entering the Church I ask the first person I see if there's someone in charge of receiving donations, and am immediately directed to the basement, where the only person there is a janitor. Actually, this is the main man at Saint Mark's, Father McCormick. He's a very cordial guy who I would never have thought was a priest because he's wearing a pair of Levi's and a sweatshirt that says 'my Father went to the Vatican and all I got was this crummy shirt.' This must be his other work uniform. It looks like he's trying to fix some plumbing fixture.

After introducing myself to him, we sit down to chat and I explain my curiosity about some checks that were given to him. I open my file and show him the dates, amounts and persons writing the checks. Father McCormick doesn't recognize any of the names as being members of his congregation, but does recall how the donations were brought in and what they were for.

A few summers ago, the Church started a program to teach swimming to many of the less fortunate kids in the neighborhood that didn't have access to a private swimming pool. They rented a nearby high school's pool and hired their own lifeguards. When they put out the word for volunteers to help teach the various levels of swimming courses, Joe Morgan came in. Because of his military background as a U.S. Navy Seal, the Church and all the kids loved to have him there. From what the Priest explained, Joe was a great swimming teacher and role model for the kids and he was terribly upset that Joe was having these present difficulties.

I ask him if he's aware that Joe isn't a Catholic, and he says that he knows Joe's a Muslim, but he still came regularly to teach the kids, and every once in a while he'd bring in a much needed donation.

All this information from the witnesses and the Priest give me a total new outlook on my client. There's certainly a lot more to him than meets the eye, and if everything I learned about these alleged bribes, along with what Vaughn told me about blasters' license complaints are true, Myra has absolutely no case against Joe other than from an anonymous phone tip and some triple hearsay from Ralph Eaton. And now that I think of it, I call Myra to ask her only one question. "Did that anonymous tip leading them to arrest Joe Morgan the first time get taped?"

Her answer is "yes," and my next call is to the high-priced rush messenger service to go downtown, pick up my copy of that call, and bring it to the boat. That tape should have been given to me prior to the prelim, but I haven't got the time to berate Myra for that now.

My autopsy guy Victor knows people who are experts at every type of criminal forensic job, and this time I have him refer me to an audio analyst. I want to hear who that anonymous tipster is and find out his identity.

You get what you pay for, or in this case, what Indovine's law firm pays for. Shortly after returning to the boat there's a knock at the hull. My tape recording has arrived.

It's on a cassette, so I pop it into my old boom box and give a listen. I don't recognize the voice. Damn! I was sure it would be Eaton's voice on that tape. Maybe he disguised his voice. The audio expert should be able to tell if it's a natural speaking voice or not, but what can we compare it to?

The heavy breathing I now hear behind me is either Laverne in an extremely good mood, or some dogmail. Attached to the dog's collar is a small micro-cassette recorder. Boy, she's good. This must be what she recorded when Eaton was in the car. There's no sense in my trying to compare the voices because I haven't got the ears or the equipment, so I call Victor's audio expert to let him know that we've got some tapes to work with.

Things are really popping along now. The phone rings and I see that it's an 847 area code, so it must be Jack B. calling from Skokie. So far, he's managed to check with the alumni association from Eaton's high school. His education was on the dealership's job application, so we had some place to start out. Unfortunately, the old broad he talked to at the school didn't remember either of the two names Jack gave her, but she said that there was a waitress over at a nearby deli that might know something about the guys.

Jack went over to the Barnum and Bagel, a popular eatery in Skokie, and located who might be a new source for information – a waitress named Phyllis Morse, who had an older brother that went to school with Eaton and Kupchic, the guy who left prints on Joe's brake tools. This is starting to get interesting. Phyllis told Jack that she seems to remember that Eaton was one of three boys who always hung around together, and their usual meeting place was Sonny's poolroom on Lawrence Avenue.

The place isn't there anymore, but Jack located the owner's son. When they got together, he told Jack that his father had the walls of the poolroom lined with pictures of the guys who hung out there, and he's sure that stored in a box somewhere, he's got a framed photo of Eaton, Kupchic, and the third member of their tight little group.

I immediately authorize Jack to spend another hundred dollars of Indovine's money to hire Sonny Berkow's son for a search of the storage container where all the photos were kept. Jack finally found the picture and says he'll Fedex it to me.

"Jack, why use Fedex, aren't you coming back here now that you found the picture?"

"Not really Mister Sharp. I rented my dream car, a Chevy Monte Carlo, and Phyllis and I want to spend some time driving around Chicago."

"That's wonderful Jack, but are you planning to stay at that luxurious place we're renting for you while you and Phyllis tour Cook County?"

"Not at all. Phyllis invited me to stay at her place. You'll really like her – she's blonde, and looks like a movie star. I'm sending a picture of her along with the Fedex package, and I'll probably see you in a couple of days."

I congratulate Jack on finding a temporary soul mate and wish him well, with the admonishment that he shouldn't make any rash decisions that might affect his life on a long-term basis.

My next call is back to Victor for another referral. This time I need a photo and computer ace that can perform the aging of faces. If the picture that Jack sends is thirty years old, we'll want to know what the players might look like today. Victor comes through again, and now I've got an Adobe Photoshop expert standing by.

Fedex just delivered Jack's package this morning and I hurriedly open it up. Sure enough, there's the sepia-toned photo of three young men, all in their early teens. There are no names attached, but I can see that one of them looks like a younger Eaton. It'll be up to the photo guy to age the others so that Victor can tell if one of them is either Kupchic or

Rosenbaum, the two low level 'wiseguys' that turned up in our fingerprint search: one on the trunk, and the other inside the trunk. I'm so busy concentrating on the framed picture that I almost don't notice the other picture that Jack sent of his new love... Miss Phyllis Morse.

I have to agree with Jack's assessment of her, because she really does look like a famous blond movie star. Unfortunately, it's Miss Piggy.

15

I've got a really busy day scheduled today. I'm dropping off the two audiocassettes at our sound guy's office, to have them compared for similarities. Then it's over to Victor's place to meet with the Photoshop guy, who'll scan in the framed photo and do his aging magic. Victor's got all the computers necessary because he does a lot of grim stuff there.

Victor's really good. He doesn't even need the photo guy to age the people in the picture. Right off the bat, he recognizes Eaton and Kupchic. I guess when you're in the corpse business you develop some recognition skills.

The pieces of the puzzle are finally starting to come together. Eaton is definitely one of the guys in the picture. The corpse in the trunk is definitely Marvin Kupchic, the safecracker. The fingerprints on the trunk of the car that Kupchic was found in belong to the third member of the group, Alan Rosenbaum. That's it. I've now placed Eaton with the dead body and the killer. Now, all I've got to do is convince Myra that she's got the wrong guy. I call her for an appointment and head over to her office.

I lay out my versions of the entire case for her.

"First, Eaton sends in a letter to the licensing boards making it look like his wife was complaining about Joe. This sets up the start of a motive. Second, he brings his safecracking buddy Kupchic to California and lets him in the dealership on several evenings while the place was closed, so that he could rig all three of the cars to explode. Third, he makes sure his wife and mother-in-law have a fatal accident in the same type of explosion that stopped the first two Suburbans. This was designed to make it look like either a product defect or serial bomber, either one would be sufficient to cover up the fact that it was all a plot to whack his wife. And, because he also knows about Joe's little bribery scam, he phones in the anonymous tip, so you can do his dirty work for him. We haven't got the voice analysis back yet, but I'm sure it'll prove that Eaton made the call to both you and to Special Agent Snell, letting the FBI know that Joe is a Muslim and that the specially painted Hummer was being worked on at the dealership before being in the Presidential July Fourth parade.

"Putting all the evidence together, not only does he get rid of his wife and her mother, he also gives up a sacrificial patsy to take the rap in both State and Federal Courts. And it's a good thing that Snell kept Joe in custody during the parade, or Eaton would have also probably framed Joe for some explosive incident there too.

"I'm not sure what happened between Kupchic and Eaton, but it probably was something about money. I'd guess that Kupchic found out how much dough Eaton was going to collect from insurance and inheritance, and he probably wanted a much bigger cut, so Eaton called his old buddy Alan

Rosenbaum, the third member of their little group, and hired him to 'off' Kupchic.

"We've already found Kupchic. He was the stiff in Stuart's Camry trunk that your boys picked up over at Victor's place. We also found his prints on some brake tools in Joe Morgan's service bay, so we have that piece of the puzzle together already.

"We also lifted Rosenbaum's prints off of the trunk that Kupchic was found in, so we can be pretty sure of that chain of events.

"We sent Jack Bibberman to Chicago on a fishing trip, and he was successful in getting a picture of all three of these losers together. Rosenbaum, Kupchic and Eaton. It's an old photo, but Victor's Photoshop expert can age Rosenbaum for you. A picture of what he probably looks like now, along with his prints, should give the locals a good chance at finding him.

"Eaton's money isn't in yet from either his wife's insurance policy or the Will, so it's a good probability that Rosenbaum's still in town waiting for his pay-off. The real good thing we've got going for us is now is surprise, because Eaton has no idea how close we are, or that I've got his whole plan figured out."

I sure hope that the rest of her office is listening in to this oratory, because it must have rivaled the best fictional detective's end-of-the-book summation. Here comes the real acid test.

"Now it's up to you, Miss District Attorney. Do you have the stones to admit that Joe Morgan is innocent, and to take this to the Grand Jury for a murder indictment of both Eaton and Rosenbaum?"

"You've done a good job of putting this together, Pete, but I still don't have enough to go against Eaton. Rosenbaum, no problem, but Eaton's the tough one."

"Myra, what are you talking about? Didn't you hear me lay out the whole case for you? Without Eaton, Rosenbaum would have no motive to kill his old friend Kupchic. If it weren't for Eaton, Rosenbaum probably wouldn't even know where Kupchic was. C'mon, you know you can do it."

"Okay Peter, I'll tell you what I will do. I'll go to the Grand Jury and get an indictment against Rosenbaum. Then we'll pick him up and sweat him a little with a capital charge hanging over his head. We'd be justified in sticking a needle in his arm because of the special circumstances here because it's a murder for hire.

"Once he's convinced we've got him cold with fingerprint evidence, maybe we can lead him to believe that Eaton gave him up and then offer to take the death penalty off of the table if he rolls on Eaton.

"It works on television. I see them do it every week on 'Law and Order,' so I don't see why we can't get away with it." Not bad. I think I've finally gotten through to her.

"Very funny. After Eaton's conviction, I can just see the headlines now, describing this case as being 'ripped from television.' Whatever. If you think it's best to do it that way, I'll go along with it.

The main thing is that my guy gets out from under the hook."

"Wait a minute, Peter. There's a small catch. Your guy has to stay in custody until we pick up Rosenbaum."

"What? You're holding my guy as ransom until you can find a replacement?"

"No, dummy, think about it. If we release him now and the word gets out, then Eaton and Rosenbaum will both know that something's going on and they may get spooked and leave town. Even if Eaton stays for the money, Rosenbaum will be gone. Seeing your guy released might even push Eaton to kill Rosenbaum. He's a loose end that Eaton can't afford to have out there.

"If he's bad enough of a guy to hire Rosenbaum to kill Kupchic, then he's certainly bad enough to hire someone to kill Rosenbaum. No, I'm sorry, but Joe Morgan can't be released yet."

"Okay Miss prosecutor, I'll tell you what. At least put him in a safe house somewhere. I'll get my client Berland to foot the bill if you'll provide the security and let Joe stay in some hotel somewhere."

Myra thinks about it for a minute.

"All right, he can stay in a hotel, but if you let word leak out that he's been released before we get a chance to grab up Rosenbaum, then the whole deal's off. Joe Morgan doesn't pass 'go' or collect two hundred dollars. He goes directly to jail."

The deal is made. I call Mister Berland to tell him that he's putting up Morgan in a hotel. He surprises me with an even better idea. He wants to

222

host Morgan at his home in Hidden Hills. It's a gated community with armed guards patrolling. I call Myra and she agrees to it. She even says that she'd like to save the expense of providing county security, so if Morgan agrees to wear an electronic anklet, he can vacation in Hidden Hills for a while. Why not? It was a good enough neighborhood for Robert Blake to stay in during his trial.

I agree to everything Myra wants and head down to the jail to give Joe Morgan the good news. I'd really like to let Indovine know that the dealership will soon be cleared of any wrongdoing, but decide to follow Myra's advice and keep the lid on everything for now.

After visiting with Joe I go back to the boat where I can sit down in comfort and put the rest of the plan together. I call Mister Berland again to finalize the arrangements. Joe will be transported to his home in an unmarked District Attorney Bureau of Investigation vehicle. Once in the house, the anklet will be attached. He's also curious about how the matter of the Will contest is going to be handled, and after explaining about Eaton's whole plan, I instruct him to continue as if none of this new info has come to light. He's to go ahead with an appraisal of all the parts of his late wife's estate, her share of the house and the business and other assets. After the appraisal is done, we'll tell Socrates Gutsue to inform Eaton's lawyer that you're ready to settle everything up in open court, at which time you'll present a cashier's check to the court in the sum of over two million.

I also tell him not to even think about liquidating anything, because no cashier's check will ever be prepared. Once Eaton's lawyer is informed that the appraisal processes are under way, all we'll have to do is call him every couple of days with new amounts in the increase to his client's share. That way he won't object to the time it's taking to finish things up. As long as his waiting time is being constantly rewarded with increases, we can buy the extra time it takes to round up Rosenbaum and connect Eaton to the deaths.

Eaton is no dummy. He knows that his luck can't last forever, and he probably can't keep Rosenbaum in hiding indefinitely, so he'll be pushing his attorney to move things along quicker. I hope that his pushing is tempered by his greed when he keeps getting informed of the increases in the amount he'll be winding up with out of probate.

This is going to be a good year for me. One real nice thing is that I've got three clients paying for my doing the same thing. If I can pull off everything planned, I can collect a reward from Berland for saving the estate from paying Eaton, from Uniman Insurance for saving them from paying Eaton, and from Indovine's firm for clearing Joe Morgan. The thing that really makes this so sweet is that it's all mine. My deal is that unless the firm is financing a case or referred it to me, I don't have to give up any portion of the money to the kid, and if I know anything about her at all, she's probably staying up nights trying to figure out some way to horn in on these fees. She really helps me out a lot on all the work, but when it's not on the law firm's matters, she bills me at a rate of thirty-five bucks an hour for administrative work, and that's okay too, because I just pass the expense on to my client. I don't feel sorry for her though, because she's already a multi-millionaire from the settlements for her mother's death in a car accident, and her stepfather's death in a plane crash. Loophole Louie, the court-appointed CPA who oversees her trust account, just sent me a statement last month. The brat is now earning a couple of hundred thousand a year in interest, but it's not all profit. I get paid one dollar a year as trustee, but I still feel in my bones she wishes I would waive the fee and do it for nothing. A typical female.

The way I have things planned, there's no way she can get a piece of the several hundred grand I'll bring in if everything comes together. Maybe I'll give her a bonus like some side curtains for her e-cart, or a big new bed for the dog. What the hell, what's money for if you can't spend a little of it on your friends?

And speaking of money, I turn in my weekly report on hours spent and expenses advanced so she can do the billing to Indovine's office and Mister Berland's company.

The phone rings. It's Jack B. and he's back from Chicago.

"Hello Romeo, how's the interstate lover doing today?"

225

"I'm fine Mister Sharp, but I'm afraid that Phyllis and I may be through. It's just too tough to maintain an interstate relationship, and neither one of us can afford to fly out to visit the other on a frequent basis."

"Oh, I'm sorry to hear that Jack. Any time you want to talk about it, I'm sure Suzi would like to counsel you."

"Yeah, maybe I'll talk to her when I'm ready. In the meantime, when I returned I found some results that came in from my inquiry to the automobile transport company. You know, the one that runs the car carrier trucks that deliver to Stuart. Per your instructions, I asked them about that one particular truck that delivered the Camry's to Stuart's place in Van Nuys. The delivery to Stuart that trip had only five Camrys on it. Their routing plan shows the truck made only two stops after picking up the five vehicles from Billy Z.'s place. The first one was in Langley, Virginia for a pickup, and the other was a delivery to the dealership where Eaton works."

I thank Jack and tell him to get an invoice over to us so we can cut him a check. The information he got is really interesting. When I spoke to some employees at the dealership they told me that whatever was off-loaded into that secure garage was done inside, and out of sight of anyone there. If my guess is correct, that wrapped-up item was probably the fancy Hummer slated to be bubble-topped and used in the parade. And if the truck dropped off the Hummer at the dealership, the first stop it made at Langley, was probably CIA Headquarters, where the

Hummer was bullet-proofed, painted, wrapped up, and loaded onto the car-carrier truck.

The driver must have gotten curious and peeked under the tarp to see what he was carrying. That must be how he knew it was the Hummer, and he probably mentioned it to Stuart, who then told Vinnie, who then told Olive, who then told me. That answers another question.

Knowing that the car-carrying truck was at the dealership also might solve another part of the puzzle, because I now think I know how Kupchic's body got into the trunk of Stuart's car.

Just for effect, I bounce my theory off of the same associate who gets to hear all my ideas... the dog. I explain to him that Eaton was letting Kupchic hide in that secure garage while he worked evenings on those Suburbans that were locked up for the night in Joe's service bay. He and Eaton had their falling out over the money, and Eaton hired Rosenbaum to kill Kupchic. The body must also have been hidden in that secure garage, so that when Eaton found out that the Hummer was being delivered, he summoned Rosenbaum to the dealership. When the car-carrier truck was backed into the garage to off-load the Hummer, Eaton distracted the truck driver while Rosenbaum dumped Kupchic's body into the trunk of one of the Camry's on the truck. The truck then delivered the Camry to Stuart's place, complete with a body in one of the trunks, and Rosenbaum's prints on the car.

I love it when a plan gets figured out so neatly. There's no disagreement from my associate, so the theory must be correct. To avoid waking the dog, I make an effort to quietly call Myra because I want to give her the new information about my recently confirmed theory. I get through to her and lay it all out. She now has all the pieces of the puzzle together, so all we have to do is get Rosenbaum and the case can be closed out. Boy, I'm good.

Stuart calls. He's bored. His Small Claims Court business is going fine and because he hired some people to make appearances, he doesn't have to work on it anymore. His used car business is going well, with several Toyota and Honda dealers buying almost everything he can bring in from Billy Z. Vinnie and Olive are now running his armored truck service and the sale of that weight control junk, so that's another responsibility off of his shoulders, and he's looking for something else to do.

I don't have any suggestions for him other than to make better use of Jack's talents as an investigator. There's a lot of insurance fraud going on out there, and defense law firms like Indovine's are always looking for good investigators to trap phony claimants. He says he'll think about it.

Most of the time the wheels of justice turn pretty slow, but with Myra's hand on the crank they spin a lot faster. I get word from the District Attorney's office that Myra went to the Grand Jury and got a murder indictment against Alan

Rosenbaum. She also had Joe Morgan released and delivered to Mister Berland's custody in Hidden Hills. Pictures of Alan Rosenbaum the way he probably looks now have been distributed to the local police agencies, and a statewide search is being conducted to find him. Wisely, Myra has held back on releasing the picture to the press, so that Eaton can be kept off guard until Rosenbaum is picked up.

My work is done for the day, so I call Berland to invite myself out to his mansion for an afternoon catered lunch. The last time I was there I noticed that he has a full time cook in the house, so I figure there'll always be something good to eat.

Joe Morgan is confused about something. He tells us that each of the first two Suburbans was towed back to his service bay for inspection and repairs. While going through them, he made a note of the mileage and also removed some extra wires that had been connected to each vehicle's odometer device.

He also noted that each of the first two vehicles had been driven the exact same number of miles before it exploded. This is a very strange coincidence, so I have Berland tell me exactly what his wife and daughter had planned for the day of their accident.

He explains that he had their driver drop his wife off at a friend's house, where she met with her weekly book group to discuss something they all recently read. His daughter was supposed to pick up her Suburban at the dealership where it had just been serviced, then pick up her mother. There was an inquiry from Las Vegas about demolition of an old hotel scheduled to be replaced, so they were both planning on taking a ride up there to get details so that a bid for the demolition could be put in. I ask him for the address where his wife's book club met and then drive over to the dealership.

With the exact mileage now known for the pre-explosion trips of the first two vehicles, I want to follow Nancy Eaton's driving path on the day of the accident and see how far she would have gotten if allowed to go that amount of miles.

The dealership's assistant manager lent me Nancy's Suburban that morning so that I could drive around to the same places that the first two owners went. What I want to do now is complete Nancy's trip by driving those extra miles, to make up for the ones that were deducted by my earlier use of the vehicle. I want to see how far she would have gotten if I hadn't used her car that morning.

The first two Suburbans didn't explode on the same day they were serviced because it took several days for each of them to accumulate the number of miles required for the explosive charges to go off.

On the day that I borrowed Nancy's Suburban, I only drove the routes that I was aware of, not knowing if any other driver of those vehicles put extra mileage on it. Today, I'm going from the dealership straight to where Mrs. Berland's book club met, and then right back to the freeway and towards Las Vegas. I'll drive the exact same number of miles as the other two Suburbans and that way I might be able to see where Eaton planned on having the explosion take place.

After about an hour of negotiating the traffic I get past the place where the accident took place and continue to the 405 Freeway, northbound. Berland told me that they were planning on taking the 'back way' to Vegas, so I drive that route until my odometer reads the same number of miles that all three Suburbans registered. I look around and don't see anything other than a deep rock quarry off to the left side of the road. We had an especially long rainy season this year, and the bottom of the quarry is filled in to create a small lake that's probably twenty feet deep.

When I first figured out what Eaton's plan might be I felt guilty that my use of her vehicle that day used up valuable miles on her odometer. If I hadn't done that, maybe she would have had that explosion in some place where the car's swerving might not have been fatal.

Now, seeing where Eaton obviously planned for the explosion to take place, I can see that all I did was make the accident happen sooner. The same results would have been there, but if it happened out here, there's a good chance that we might not discover it for months, if ever.

Thinking back, now I understand why Eaton was so mad at his assistant manager for letting me borrow that vehicle. If not for the fact that it ultimately went off of Mulholland Drive, his plan might have failed completely, with just a minor traffic collision. That would have been a tremendous inconvenience to him, because he probably already had Rosenbaum kill Kupchic, so there would be no one left to rig her vehicle a second time.

Back at the boat, I think I hear a small crowd gathering out on the dock. It must be haircut day. Once every month or so, the kid gives Bernie a touch-up trim. She can't reach the top of his head, so after she gets him to sit down, she stands on a milk crate and uses her Flowbee with a vacuum attachment to give his fur an always-needed trimming. It's really an amazing device. First, you adjust the length that you want the hair to remain. Then you plug in the Flowbee, turn on its vacuum attachment, and gently pass it over whatever hairy surface you want to trim. She also has some battery-operated flea-killing comb that she passes over him a couple of times. It's something she ordered from the Sharper Image catalog.

There aren't many adults on the dock who request a Flowbee trim, but when people in the adjoining apartment buildings see her start to trim Bernie, they all send their kids down for a Flowbee freebie. The kids love it because not only do they get their locks trimmed, they also get to hang onto Bernie.

16

The messenger service is here again and this time it's with attorney Larkin's answer to the Interrogs I sent to his office. Opening the package disappoints me. Not only did they answer every question without objection, they dotted each i and crossed each t. Damn them. Now I have no reason to drag them into court with objections and I've lost a good stall tactic.

Our office already filed my Answer with the court, so they have no chance at a default judgment. I'm going to have to think of some way to stall this case until Myra's people grab Rosenbaum. I guess the best way is to schedule a deposition, so I instruct our office to start the subpoena process.

The phone rings. It's Socrates Gutsue and he's not happy. The Probate Court is moving ahead and pretty soon it's going to be judgment day, when we have to appear and Mister Berland will have to deposit a huge some of money with the court so that they can distribute it per the instructions in his late wife's will. Eaton will become wealthy and disappear, and Berland will be out several million dollars. I can't let this happen, but until Rosenbaum is caught, there's not much I can do.

The kid comes out of her domain and picks up Eaton's Interrog answers. I don't have the slightest idea what she wants with them, but since they didn't give me any information that would help me, I don't care what happens to that pile of paper. She'll probably go through every answer, in an attempt to build up her billable hours.

Myra's office sends an email putting me on notice that the Grand Jury murder indictment they have against Rosenbaum is not a perpetual thing, and that if they don't apprehend him before this Grand Jury's term expires, they'll have to pick up Joe Morgan again. They obviously don't want to be without someone to blame the murders on.

From the looks of things, the clock is now ticking again. If I don't come up with something soon, Eaton will get away with murder, and a lot of money.

It's not over yet. Another messenger is knocking on the hull with a thick package from Larkin's office. Opening it up, I see the most extensive set of Interrogatories and Request for Admissions I've ever seen. If I don't figure out some way to end this mess soon, I'll be forced to hire the kid for the better part of a full week to organize the answers this jerk wants. I see that a lot of those questions pertain to the value of our boat, so he's obviously going for punitive damages and wants to know everything I've got so he can go after it. I'm sure that when the kid sees that they've got their eyes on the boat, she'll become more motivated to do them in.

I think we'll be having a big dinner tonight. Of course nobody's said anything to me yet, but the crowd is growing by the hour. First it was Jack, who spent some time with the princess in a counseling session, probably due to his loss of consortium with Miss Piggy. Then it was Vinnie and Olive, probably here for marriage therapy. Now Stuart is in there, no doubt getting helped with his correspondence law school homework. I wish there was some way that I could make an appointment to get in there and be told how to find Alan Rosenbaum.

There's another knock at the hull. Vinnie goes to see who it is and invites our new visitor aboard. It's Victor, and while he's here to pick something up from Suzi, he gets invited to stay for dinner too.

As long as it's going to be a party, I might as well have a date, so I send a dogmail message to Laverne, inviting her to join us and bring a large can of her favorite wine. After a strenuous evening of conversation I'll probably spend the night on her houseboat, so she might as well be here to walk back with me. I intend to have an extra few drinks with dinner and Laverne will be my guide back to her place.

The phone rings. It's Mister Berland calling to see if there are any new developments on the case. After I make my no-news report, he asks about the noise he hears in the background. I tell him that there are about nine or ten of us getting ready to have dinner in an hour or so. He asks if he can join us.

"Sure, Mister Berland, it would be our pleasure to have you here with us, but you're supposed to be a full-time babysitter with your guest. Remember? The D.A. doesn't want him left alone."

"Well, Peter, then why don't you all come out here? My chef can whip up a gourmet meal for all of us. And if it makes matters any easier, I'll send two stretch limos for all of you, so no designated driver will be necessary. And I'll bet my wine cellar is better than yours."

I tell the group about Berland's invitation and they all think it would be fun to go out there in the limos. Laverne, having been informed that she may be going to a location where there's a genuine wine cellar, makes the final decision for all of us. I tell Berland to send the limos and Suzi calls to cancel the Asian boys' delivery. She also calls Myra to invite her along, but being the pro that she is, Myra respectfully declines, explaining to the kid that it really wouldn't be proper for her to be at a dinner party with a person who she has a current file against. Too bad, but she's right.

The evening is a success. July is a hot month in most of the country, and especially so in the west San Fernando Valley where Hidden Hills is situated. By the time that the limos get us all there, the sun has already set, so the stifling heat is gone, and we decide to dine outdoors between the huge swimming pool and the large brick barbeque, where Berland's chef is preparing charcoal broiled swordfish and spare ribs. There's also no shortage of side dishes.

The food is great, the conversation is interesting, and Berland has two large German shepherd guard dogs, so Bernie has some new friends. They're are on their best behavior with everyone at the dinner party, but I'm sure they can be a force to reckon with for any uninvited guest.

The limos bring us all back to the Marina, Suzi has a large doggie bag, and I'm going for a backrub and whatever other options are available at casa Laverne.

The sun is shining and I'm finishing up my last slice of greasy French toast. The houseboat rocks a little as the dogmail carrier steps aboard with a note for me. It's a message that came in from Socrates Gutsue's office, putting us on notice that we only have another day or two to either get the goods on Eaton or let him have his inheritance.

I've always hated working against a ticking clock, but this time there's nothing I can do about it. I make my usual morning call to Myra's office to learn whether or not there's any progress in finding Rosenbaum. The probate court date is rapidly approaching and I can already feel those huge checks slipping out of my hand.

Indovine calls to let me know that Uniman can't stall any more. The death benefit on Eaton's wife must be paid soon, because it if isn't, the insurance company will be exposing itself to a large bad-faith lawsuit from Eaton. I tell him that we'll try to wrap it up soon. I don't even believe it myself as I say the words.

I make the usual round of calls to Victor, Jack B., Vaughn, our photo guy and our sound guy. The audio expert has some news. He's completed the comparison analysis between the two tapes and he's prepared to testify that the anonymous tipster is none other than Ralph Eaton. I thank him very much and call Myra with the news. She's glad to hear that another part of my theory has been confirmed, but correctly states our position as still being the same. Without Rosenbaum, we've got nothing... nada, zip, zilch, zero, gournisht. I'm glad to hear that her international thesaurus is still working.

Only one more day until Larkin and Eaton are triumphant. I hate to lose, especially to a jerk attorney and a murderer. The only upside will be that once Eaton has the money and leaves the country, he won't want to continue with his groundless defamation suit against me.

I make the usual calls to everyone concerned and for once I know what it must feel like for a candidate to make a concession speech after seeing that the election didn't go his way.

The other line rings. This is private line reserved for Suzi's incoming calls. I see it's Victor calling for some reason or another, probably to ask the kid for autopsy advice. Why not? She obviously knows everything there is to know in this world.

Mister Berland won't be hurt too much because he wouldn't have gotten his wife's share of the estate anyway – it was earmarked for charities. He's really not happy that Eaton will get it all, and he's even more depressed that his new friend and houseguest will be taken back to jail. Berland makes a very nice gesture, but I have to tactfully explain that spiriting Joe Morgan out of the country and to some safe place with no extradition laws is not the right thing to do. I hope he takes my advice.

I'm sitting here in the boat's dining area drowning in my own self-pity when I hear two sounds of pitter-patter. They're both on their way to her stateroom, and as she passes by me I hear her mutter something. At first, it doesn't register, so I call out to her just as she's about to close her door. "What did you say?"

She answers quickly as she slams her door shut. "I know where Rosenbaum is."

17

This is the last straw. I can't take it any more. She can't possibly know where Rosenbaum is. Who does she think she is, Nero Wolfe? She hasn't done any investigation. All she's done is listen to my conversations with everyone else. If there's anything she knows, I must know it too, but I just don't know that I know it.

I also know there's no use trying to get the information out of her unless she's willing to part with it, so I decide to send her a message. To attract the messenger I shake the box of his dog biscuits. Getting in his way while he's heading for the box is probably as dangerous as trying to stop a guy like Shaquille O'Neal while he's running at full speed toward the backboard.

Once the drooling messenger has arrived, I neatly place a biscuit in his mouth and a note in his collar. My message to her contains only four words, which are no doubt the only ones she wants to hear. "What do you want?"

The messenger returns to her domain and if I know this kid at all, she's got a whole laundry list of demands prepared, on top of which is the law firm's taking jurisdiction of my reward fees. I knew she would come up with some way to get a piece of me on this one.

My answer comes in the form of another e-mail from her. First, she wants our law firm to share in all the fees and rewards earned for stopping Eaton from collecting on the insurance and the inheritance. Second, she wants to personally arrange to have Rosenbaum in the probate courtroom on judgment day, so that the whole cast of characters is assembled. As much as I don't care for the first two demands, her next ones are even tougher. She wants to be the one who fingers Rosenbaum, because she claims to be the only person involved in this case who knows what he actually looks like now.

The last demand is the real deal-buster. She wants to bring the dog to court with her.

I don't have a very good track record when it comes to dealing with this kid, so figuring that anyone else in the world would have a better chance with her, I fax the demand letter to Myra, with only one added comment. "This message was mistakenly sent to my inbox. Obviously it's meant for you."

I can't ignore the coincidence. Victor called her on the private line just before she made that remark to me and sent the demand letter.

I call Victor. He hasn't the slightest idea of what I could possibly be talking about. I knew it. She bought him off. Now she's in complete control.

Myra calls me. It took a few minutes longer than I expected. I answer with a complete absence of small talk

"Yeah I know, she's out of her mind. Are you going to take care of this, or not? I don't care one way or the other. I've put a lot of energy into this case, and I think that since you're the District Attorney, the top law officer in this county, it's your job to interrogate her. Personally, I suggest a thumbscrew, but if your department is out of them, maybe a stretching rack would do the trick."

"Calm down, Peter. She's obviously cracked the case and wants to help us, but we have to help her too."

"Help her? Help her? She's holding us all captive unless she gets a ransom payment, and it's coming out of my pocket! And we both know there's no way we can allow her to bring that small horse into court with her, and that's to say nothing of the possible danger of the situation. If she's right, there's going to be a killer in that courtroom. No way. I won't allow it."

"Okay Peter, just chill. If you really know her as well as you think you do, then you'll have to agree that there's no way she'll lose a share of the bonus fees by letting that money go to Eaton, and she's working you like a slot machine. Can't you see that?"

"Sure I see that. So what makes this day different from other days of the year? She's always playing me like a jukebox, but this time she's got something that we all need very badly. Hell, the People of the State of California need her information. There's a murderer on the loose out there and this may be our only chance to get him. Myra, you've got to talk some sense into her."

"Okay, Peter, I'll give it a shot, but I can't make any promises. You know she's got a mind of her own."

Yeah, I know she's got a mind of her own. The thing that really gets to me is that it's so much better than mine. She can't possibly know any more about this case than I do, so how can she figure it out when I can't? Myra's no dummy either, and the kid's beat her to the solution too. Maybe my fate is to just follow her around and chronicle her cases, like Doctor John Watson did for Sherlock Holmes. Please, just shoot me now.

The day has arrived. I'm on my way to the probate court. I've had no luck with the kid and neither has Myra. I can't believe I'm going down in flames like this today. I've let everyone down, from Indovine and Uniman, to Joe Morgan and Mister Berland. Everyone looked to me for a miracle. I was supposed to pull a rabbit out of my hat. Even Myra was hoping I could pull it off and give her a really good convictable person. It's all going down the tubes. In another hour or so, Larkin will be sneering at me, Mister Berland will be poorer, Joe Morgan will be back in jail, and Eaton will be a multi-millionaire.

Losing the bonus fees and getting embarrassed isn't the worse though, it'll be seeing Joe Morgan, an innocent guy, get thrown back into County Jail and forced to stand trial for two murders that I know he didn't commit.

For some strange reason Suzi refuses to ride to court with me. She says she has something else planned. I'm afraid to ask what it is, so I leave the boat and meet Jack at the Hummer for our drive downtown.

Entering the courtroom, I see that it's packed. There's a full house, including attorney Socrates Gutsue, Charles Indovine, Mister Uniman, Mister Berland, Victor, Stuart, Vinnie and Olive, Myra, some reporters, and about six uniforms. Something's going on here and I wish I knew what it is. I'll bet the kid invited everyone so she can have a big audience for whatever bone-headed stunt she intends to pull off.

I keep looking around the courtroom, but don't see any faces I haven't seen before. If the kid's running this show properly, then Rosenbaum should be here too.

The courtroom doors swing open and everyone inside watches as Eaton and Larkin strut in. Their coming in reminds me of how I once watched Hulk Hogan and the Rock make grand entrances to those ridiculous wrestling matches drawing millions on pay-per-view. It's all showbiz, and now Eaton's part of it. He and Larkin take their sweet time getting to the counsel table. They turn around and smirk at the crowd, letting everyone know that they've won and the rest of us are all losers.

Unlike the Federal Courtrooms, State Court time runs on the judge's watch. When he feels like

246

coming out, the court session begins. If he doesn't come out, it's just a room full of nervous people sitting and looking at each other.

The courtroom doors open again and this time it's Special Agent Snell and his flunkies coming in. I can't figure out why he's here, but what the hell, everyone else is, so why shouldn't the FBI come and watch me being made a fool of?

It's an afternoon session, and the clock on the wall shows just another minute or two before court is normally scheduled to begin. The court clerk makes an announcement that the judge will be a little late, so we should all just stick around until he arrives.

This isn't the normal course of events. As clever as the kid is, I can't possibly believe that her powers are so far-reaching as to make a judge come to court late.

What seems like an hour passes by, but the clock on the wall says it was only two minutes. The double courtroom doors open again and I sit in complete disbelief at what I see starting to come in. It's the kid, and she's wearing a pair of dark sunglasses, walking very slowly into the room and is accompanied by the Saint Bernard, who's wearing one of those harnesses that seeing-eye dogs wear. This can't be happening. She's actually trying to pass herself off as a blind person with a Saint Bernard seeing-eye dog.

I lean forward on the counsel table and want to hide my head in my hands until this whole thing is over. I'd much rather prefer finding a loose piece of carpet to crawl under, but hiding my head in my hands will just have to do for now. But, like a car wreck on the freeway or a car chase on the local news, I'm drawn to what's happening and can't turn away.

I look over towards Eaton. He obviously recognizes her as the little kid that was in the back seat of the Hummer that day we spoke. He must remember having made some incriminating remarks while in the car with us, and for an instant I think I see some apprehension on his face. Both he and Larkin realize that what's happening right now in this courtroom has probably never happened before and will never happen again, and nothing good will come of it.

As the kid and dog approach the partition separating participants from spectators, a bailiff opens the swinging gate and the two of them start through. At the same time, out of the corner of my eye, I see Myra, Snell, and all the uniformed officers getting up and starting to follow the kid.

I'm not going to bail her out of this one. She's finally lost it. After they arrest her for this crazy stunt, it'll take an enormous donation to get her into any decent college or law school, and I'm not going to come up with one cent in contribution. She's going to get busted and I don't care. She's bringing it all upon herself, so I'm just going to sit back and watch. Actually, it's kind of nice seeing her make a fool out of herself. I've been doing it for years, so it's about time she learned what it's like to fall completely flat on your face in a court of law, with everyone you know watching. It'll be a learning experience for her.

The show's not over yet. Once through the rail, she and the dog slowly approach the other counsel table, and then it happens. The kid reaches down to the dog's collar and removes a blue-backed piece of paper. She holds it up in the air and looks like she's preparing to make an announcement of some sort. There's a hush in the courtroom. By now, some reporters have come through the back doors, and cameras are at the ready.

This isn't possible. There are no cameras allowed in here. The kid nods towards the cameras and their battery powered lights come on, bathing her in the spotlight. She waves the blue-backed document in the air, looks directly at Eaton and says, "Alan Rosenbaum, I have in my hand a copy of the Grand Jury Indictment, calling for your arrest on the charges of the pre-meditated murder of Nancy Eaton, Estelle Berland, and Marvin Kupchic. In addition, you will be charged with federal crimes involving explosives.

Larkin is sitting there in a state of shock. Eaton looks around like he wants to make a break for it. The kid shouts out "book 'em boys." At this point, Eaton jumps back away from her and towards the private exit that the judge uses, but it's no use. The court's bailiff is there to block him and the six uniforms grab him. They struggle him to the ground, and once he's cuffed they drag him away.

I'm standing up at this point, and as she and the dog slowly walk past me towards the cameras, I can see down behind her dark glasses that she's winking at me. Myra, who is now standing next to me, tells me to close my mouth because it's hanging open a little too far.

On her way to the cameras for her moments of fame, she passes by Indovine and Mister Uniman. They chat for a brief moment and Uniman removes an envelope from his inside coat pocket and hands it to her. Next, she passes by Mister Berland, who also hands her an envelope. After collecting my bonuses, she walks out into the hallway to be interviewed.

I still don't believe what just happened here, especially without the judge walking out to see what the commotion was, so I go over to Mary, the court clerk.

"Mary, would you please tell me how you succeeded in getting the judge to stay in chambers while this circus act was being performed?"

"Oh Mister Sharp, that was no problem. The judge isn't here today. He's attending a judicial conference in Santa Barbara. It was calendared over a month ago."

"But I don't understand. How could you schedule all of our appearances on a day when the judge wasn't going to be here?"

"There were no appearances scheduled for today. Your office manager called and asked if both sides could use the courtroom to discuss a settlement. I checked with the judge and he said it was okay with him. He wasn't going to be here and didn't care what went on, as long as you guys didn't make too much of a mess."

I can see that the kid has been busy for the past few days. I wonder how long she knew about Eaton's alleged double identity before clueing me in on it. I still don't know if she's right about it, but if she isn't, we'd better find a new place to live, because Eaton and Larkin will own a nice fifty-foot Grand Banks.

On my way out of the courtroom I stop to chat for a minute with Indovine and Uniman. Charles calls me aside and thanked me.

"Peter, you're a true gentleman. When your little office manager came by to pick up your bonus, she made sure to tell Mister Uniman that all your efforts were directed and supported by my office."

"No problem, Charles. Now that you know I can be trusted to do the right thing, maybe this could be the start of a nice business relationship. By the way, how come the both of you just happened to be here today?"

"Oh, that was set up last week by the little one. We exchanged faxes until the exact terms of your bonus was agreed upon, and then she told us when and where to show up. She's very good, you know."

I didn't waste my time asking Snell what brought him to court today. The answer would no doubt have been a re-play of what I just heard from Indovine and Uniman. I'm sure that Snell's main interest was in finding out for sure that there was no plan to harm the President during that parade.

Almost at the same time that the uniforms are escorting Eaton out of the courtroom, another person comes walking in. Its Joe Morgan. He tells me that Myra arranged for all charges to be dropped but requested that he stay out of Eaton's view until the arrest was made. I guess everyone was in on this show but me.

Standing just inside the double doors is Myra, obviously waiting for the kid to finish her little press conference so that maybe the cameras will then turn in the direction of the District Attorney.

"You were in on this whole plan, weren't you Myra?"

"If I remember correctly, you told me to handle it, didn't you?"

"Yeah, but I didn't ask you to help me get blindsided. That brat went completely around me. She took over this whole courtroom, arranged to stage this event when she knew the judge would be out of town, and even went so far as to get his permission to use the place. She made sure that everyone involved was here, including my civil defense law firm client, his client, the FBI, you, uniformed cops, and the press. It would have been nice if you would've given me a little heads-up on what was going to go down here today. Maybe I would have worn my good suit."

"You're right, Pete, it would have been nice, but there was only one way she was going to help us all out, and it was under the condition that it was done exactly the way she planned it, and that meant not saying anything to you. But while you're

252

complaining, you should face the facts. There was only a day or so remaining before Eaton would have gotten all the money and disappeared forever. If that happened, who knows what a jury would have done to your client Joe Morgan? Face it Pete, the kid saved all our asses, and it's a happy ending all the way around, so stop whining about your ego getting bruised."

"Yeah, okay. Here comes the bailiff. Probably another little surprise the kid's arranged."

The bailiff hands me a note. "It's from that little Asian girl. She wanted me to hand it to you after she went out into the hallway." I open the note and see that it's another request for my services. "We need a ride home, please. Bernie and I took a cab here." At least she said please.

18

Why not? She's already stolen the day, solved the crime, saved the insurance company and Berland's estate, pulled Joe Morgan out of the fire, and confiscated a good portion of my bonuses. I'm obviously good for nothing else but being her chauffeur, so I might as well get used to it.

There is the usual amount of conversation in the car on the way back to the Marina. The only thing I say is "nice job."

Her response is "watch my news conference when they broadcast it tonight."

She knows that I was in the courtroom all the while she was being interviewed by the press, and she wants to make sure that I see her entire performance. I know better than to ask her any questions, so I just keep my mouth shut and keep driving.

When we're just a mile or so away from the Marina, she points to one of our favorite Mexican Restaurants, the Pollo Meshuga, and says "pull up over there."

Now what? She probably wants to stop in for drink to celebrate her victory and my failure. I park the Hummer and leave the windows open for Bernie's comfort, and we walk into the restaurant. By now, she's shed the sunglasses, which I overheard her tell Myra were mainly for the bright lights from the camera. What a little ham she is.

We open the door and enter the restaurant and are greeted by everyone we know, who all stand up and applaud our entrance. The kid purposely stalled during her press conference, in order to give everyone a chance to get here before us. We're greeted at the door by Socrates Gutsue, who helps us all get seated. He tells me that Indovine's firm arranged to have Joe Morgan promoted to assistant manager at the dealership. The assistant was moved up to take Eaton's place, and Joe was given all the back pay he missed, plus a big bonus for the inconvenience he went through. It's Joe who's paying for the party, having worked it all out with the kid during the past two days.

Once we're all seated the crowd quiets down, and Hector turns the television sets to an English-speaking channel so that we can all watch the evening news.

Naturally, what happened in court today is the lead story, and there she is on the screen, surrounded by the reporters with a bunch of microphones in front of her. She must have been coached by Myra for this performance, because she pulled it off perfectly. A bunch of questions were shouted at her, but she only made a brief statement. "Thank you all for coming, but I didn't really do anything. I sat back and watched my legal guardian, attorney Peter Sharp, do all the work. With the help of District Attorney Myra Scot and FBI Special Agent Robert Snell, along with the financial and legal assistance of the Charles Indovine law firm and Uniman Insurance, all the facts were brought in, and I'm glad that they let a kid like me help out. I'm sorry for bringing my dog into the courtroom today. Peter and Myra told me it was against the rules, but he was with me during the whole case, and the cab driver wouldn't let him wait in the cab, so I had to bring him in with me."

That was the end of the news conference. I even saw tears in some of the eyes in the room that evening. The most heard words from the reporters and onlookers included 'adorable,' 'cute,' and 'bright little girl.' If they only knew. I do give her a lot of credit though, for her political savvy. She knows that I front for the firm, Myra is the top law official in Los Angeles County, and Snell is the local FBI bureau chief, so she generously spread the credit around, and didn't forget to let Charles Indovine share in it too. I'm sure that'll bring us more business.

I make sure to let her know that after the party she will either tell me how she cracked the case, or instead of bringing her back to the boat with me I will be dropping her off at the nearest orphanage, and leaving Bernie at the pound.

We all party on for the next couple of hours until the kid reminds us that it's past her bedtime, so everyone decides to call it quits. She even took control of the party. It's wonderful to see how she can manipulate the world like that.

On the way back to the boat, she tells me that a full report is waiting for me in my email, and that if it doesn't answer all my questions, she'll try to explain it to me tomorrow. Then, like the little drama queen that she is, she lets me know that "it's been a long day. "Bernie and I have to go to sleep."

True to her word, there is a full report on my computer screen. It's a short one, less than one page long.

Peter:

You did a good job of gathering the information, but the one thing you completely neglected was to dig a little deeper. Here's what you missed.

1. Eaton's social security number was on his job application at the dealership, but you never ran it through.

2. You knew that both Kupchic and Rosenbaum had arrest records, but you neglected to have the police agencies send you their mug shots

3. You missed the fact that Eaton didn't have a Car Salesman's license, which means he was never required to have his fingerprints taken and put on record.

4. You made a false assumption when Jack B. gave us that picture of Eaton, Rosenbaum and Kupchic. You mistakenly believed which one was Eaton, with absolutely no supporting evidence to back it up.

I did all the things you neglected to do. The final solution to the case came when Eaton's lawyer sent over the answers to the Interrogs you gave them. I knew that Eaton would have to sign them, so I gave them to Victor to dust for prints. The results were a match for only two people – Larkin, who was printed before taking the Bar exam, and Rosenbaum. That's when I knew he wasn't Eaton.

With Snell's help, we ran Eaton's social security number through and discovered that Ralph Eaton was killed in action while serving in Viet Nam. The final clinchers were the mug shots of both

257

Rosenbaum and Kupchic, sent to us by the Chicago Police Department.

"I apologize for grandstanding the way I did, but you do it all the time and I wanted to see what it's like.

All things taken into consideration, I have to admit that she was right on every point. It's all a matter of perspective, and if I didn't have the responsibility of a capital murder case on my hands, maybe I would have done better. After all, the only thing she had to concentrate on was finding my mistakes. Still, she did a good job and I'm proud of her.

Jack B. called and thanked me for the generous bonus he received in the mail, and Father McCormick called to thank me for helping Joe out of trouble.

Mister Berland called to let me know that Joe's licenses came through, so now he's a licensed 'powder man' and can work on every type of job that his company gets, so he'll be using Joe as much as he can.

I never heard from the owner of the dealership, but if he ever sobers up long enough to read about the case, maybe he'll call too.

As for the kid and me, I guess we'll just continue with our peaceful coexistence and she'll keep on running my life and solving my cases. One thing that I did to try and maintain some level of control is to store the big bags of dog food in a cabinet up on the boat's flybridge. She's reluctant to use the access ladder, so she now needs me at least once a week to go up there and fetch for her.

The mail was just delivered. I opened only one of the two pieces – it's from Stuart, inviting us to an office party for the opening of his new private investigation agency. The other one I won't open because it's addressed to the kid. It's from Harvard Law School.

———◆———

The Peter Sharp Legal Mystery Series

#1: *Single Jeopardy*

Attorney Peter Sharp has been wrongfully suspended from the practice of law and thrown out of the house by his soon-to-be ex-wife, a newly appointed deputy district attorney. As a result of the eviction, he's forced to live in their back yard on an old, poorly wired, 40-foot Chris Craft cabin cruiser he's restoring, that is in danger of burning up at any time.

To make matters worse, as the result of trying to help someone fill out some claim forms, he gets arrested for conspiracy to defraud an insurance company. His alleged co-conspirator, a man charged with murdering his own wife to be with a beautiful flight attendant, is about to discover that Peter is also sleeping with her while the man is out of town.
As Peter fights to get his law license reinstated, he discovers the secrets behind two murders, a fatal plane crash, and who framed him with the State Bar - all with the help of his legal ward Suzi, an adorable, quiet (at least to Peter) ten-year-old Chinese girl and her huge Saint Bernard.

Peter also gets involved in matters concerning sexual harassment, vexatious litigation, double jeopardy, and a groundbreaking case of *Negligent Nymphomania.*

#2: *...By Reason of Sanity*

In his second Adventure, Attorney Peter Sharp gets retained to defend a man accused of capital murder. The only things making this case a little harder to defend than most others are that the client's acts were captured on videotape, he confessed to the police, and he wants to plead guilty. To make matters worse, the District Attorney's office has brought in a special prosecutor for the trial: Peter's ex-wife Myra.

While he's preparing for trial on the murder case, Peter is also hired to represent an insurance company, to defend it against a man who slipped and fell while inside a bank that was coincidentally robbed later that same day. Peter thinks the case would have died when the claimant was murdered, but at usual, he's wrong.

In this adventure, while Peter is involved representing Vinnie, the prolific, peeing pornographer, he also helps solve several bank robberies by catching the entire gang, and makes the acquaintance of a new friend who runs an autopsy store - all with the help of his legal ward, the adorable ten-year-old Suzi and her huge Saint Bernard.

#3: *A Class Action*

In his third Adventure, Attorney Peter Sharp is retained to represent a man accused of murder, by the planting of bombs in vehicles. The client is also suspected of being part of a conspiracy to assassinate the President of the United States in an upcoming Fourth of July parade.

With the assistance of his legal ward Suzi, Peter cracks the case, identifies the real murderer, and at the same time solves the mystery of a dead body found in his friend Stuart's automobile trunk... all while falling for a lesbian lawyer, winning a Will contest, breaking up a stolen car ring 4,000 miles away, and battling with his ex-wife, who has been elected to the office of District Attorney.

In the adventure's finale, Suzi miraculously manages to get 'Bernie,' her huge Saint Bernard into a courtroom, where she makes her first official court appearance, holds her first press conference, and becomes a local television hero.

#4: *"Conspiracy of Innocence"*

Suzi once again saves Peter's case by finding the connection between two crimes that allegedly took place in different parts of the State, one of which Peter was arrested for. And once again, Peter falls for a woman who he thinks could really 'be the one' this time.

Peter's ex-wife Myra must make the decision as to whether or not she should resign from prosecution of a case in which she may have a conflict of interest – Peter's murder charge.

Everyone including Peter is sitting on the edge of their chairs as this double murder mystery comes to a shocking conclusion that involves a mafia hit man, revengeful drug dealers, a local police chief, and the ever-popular FBI.

#5: ...*Until Proven Innocent*

Tony Edwards, A dock neighbor of Peter's, is charged with murder. Unfortunately, he is a suspended police officer with a known dislike for people who are the color of his alleged victim. He's also the subject of many citizen complaints for using excessive force in the minority community.

At Suzi's request, Tony has taught her how to help him re-load his target practice ammunition, also giving the little girl a basic course in ballistics.

When a local black movie producer who Tony was working for gets killed, Suzi and talks Peter into handling Tony's defense... which doesn't look too good because he was arrested at the scene of the murder with his gun still smoking.

Along the way, Peter once again gets involved with who he thinks might be 'Miss Right,' represents a 500-pound woman who is being discriminated against, uncovers a white supremist militant organization, and also stumbles onto a group of people who are pirating DVD copies of recently released major motion pictures.

Peter's ex-wife, District Attorney Myra Scot, makes a mistake when she subpoenas little Suzi to come and testify as a prosecution witness against the defendant, Suzi's friend Tony.

After what Suzi does to solve the mystery and destroy Myra's case in court, everyone knows that the District Attorney's office will never subpoena Suzi again.

#6: *The Common Law*

Peter Sharp encounters a client with amnesia, who not only can't tell Peter what his own name is, but who also has absolutely no recollection of the crime he is charged with committing. In lieu of his memory, Peter's obtains video surveillance footage that establishes his client's guilt beyond a reasonable doubt.

The usual crew also gets involved, including Peter's close friend Stuart, Jack Bibberman the investigator, Laverne the 'amorous houseboat lady', and Stuart's employees Vinnie and Olive – who are having some disagreement as to whether or not they're legally married; and last but not least, little Suzi B. and her big Saint Bernard.

The law firm is still operating from their 50-foot Grand Banks trawler yacht in Marina del Rey, California… the vessel that Peter still doesn't know how to drive. As in past adventures, all involved continue to visit the local haunts.

One way or another each of Peter's cases winds up being a conflict with his ex-wife Myra, who is the county's chief prosecutor. He also may be more closely involved with FBI Special Agent in Charge Bob Snell than before, as they share a dangerous high-speed situation on a winding road.   Suzi's new friend Lotus and her mother also play an interesting part in this adventure as Peter finds that he is fighting a ring of credit-card fraud experts.

#7: *The Magician's Legacy*

Little Suzi has decided that she wants to study magic in this eighth legal adventure she participates in. Unfortunately, her teacher is the main suspect in what appears to be an 'impossible' crime... the shooting of a man in his completely locked 'safe room.'

In order for Suzi to clear her magic teacher of liability for this crime, she must convince Peter to handle the case, which he does under one condition: Suzi must help him by solving the mystery of this locked-room murder.

Her task is made difficult because all events took place in a secure 'panic room,' with steel doors in place, and no windows. Somehow, the alleged murderer is believed to have committed the crime and successfully escaped from a room that could only later be opened by a crew using blowtorches.

Suzi is especially motivated to solve this enigma when she learns that an attorney who she dislikes may be involved.

#8: *The Reluctant Jurist*

There's a mini flu epidemic going around in Los Angeles and it has especially taken its toll among Superior Court Judges in Santa Monica, who all seem to have been infected at the same conference they attended.

Peter has been 'drafted' to fill in as a temporary judge for some civil matters, but winds up getting stuck hearing a big criminal trial involving a devious attorney as the defendant... the same attorney who Peter crossed swords with in a previous situation.

Suspense enters the picture when Peter's legal ward Suzi fails to appear as guest of honor at her own birthday party, and every local state and Federal peace officer in California wants to locate her.

This is the second adventure that Peter and Suzi B. have been involved where Suzi's Saint Bernard may be partly responsible for a successful conclusion.

#9: *The Final Case*

Suzi dislikes a certain devious attorney who Peter keeps coming up against.

When Peter's new romantic interest invites him to a cocktail party, Suzi and the other guests are shocked by a loud noise down the hall, coming from their host's study.

Other guests at the party include the chief of police, mayor, and district attorney, who unanimously conclude that the dead body they discover is the result of a suicide.

Even Suzi is inclined to go along with their conclusion... until she learns that the devious attorney she dislikes may be involved in handling some legal matters for the deceased.

Suzi won't let go of this one. Against everyone's advice, she keeps working to prove her suspicions about that devious attorney and his connections to what Suzi believes must have been murder.

All thirteen of the Peter Sharp Legal Mysteries are now available at bookstores and can easily be ordered from Ingram Book Group or Baker & Taylor book distributors. They are also available online from Amazon in print various e-book versions.

To order at your local bookseller or online, simply provide the title's ISBN (International Standard Book Number), or insert it into Amazon's search block.

For full details see **www.LegalMystery.com**

Editor's note:

If you happen to notice any blatant typographical errors in the text of this book, we suggest you bring them to the attention of the author, who was the last person to sign off on the manuscript. We feel quite comfortable shifting the blame onto him for any errors he may have missed. He can be reached through editor@MagicLampPress.com

About the Author

Gene Grossman worked his way through high school, college, and law school as a shoe salesman, welder, process server, bail bondsman, tire changer, saloon piano player and 'extra,' appearing in seven motion pictures. He then spent 20 years as a trial lawyer, during which time he served as Dean of a small local law school, and taught several classes.

The film and video company he started while working in the motion picture industry produced over fifty special interest DVD titles on everything from boating, to bankruptcy. Now retired from the practice of law, Gene writes aboard his yacht in Marina del Rey, California.

You can see pictures of attorney Peter Sharp's boats, yellow Hummer, Suzi's e-cart, Bernie, and Laverne's houseboat at **www.PeterSharpBooks.com**